A
PLIM
FROM
MARS

SHINJI PARK

ShinJi Park was born in 1991 in Busan, South Korea. She entered Nam-Cheon Primary School in 1998. While she stayed with her family in England for two years(2000~2002), she attended Christ Church C. of E. Junior School(New Malden London) and St. Mary's Catholic Primary school(Leek, Staffordshire). While studying, she received an excellent essay award. After she returned Korea with her family, she attended Busan International Middle School(2004~2006) and Busan International High School(2007~2009). Also she was an excellent student at Korea University Department of English Language and Literature(2010~2013). From childhood, she loved reading books and writing essays. As result, she received several awards in writing essays.

She wrote these marvellous stories in this book while she stayed in England for two years. When she created these stories with her heartful imagination, she was between eleven and twelve years old only. So, the background of this book is from 2000 to 2002. Previously, she had already published a book. The title of the book is 'THE WONDERFUL STORY CLUB'.

This book contains more interesting stories that were not included in the first book. The whole story contains what she wrote as a very young child. In addition, an appendix contains what she wrote when she was university student. She wrote these articles when she was a reporter of 'Korea University English Magazine'.

A PLIM FROM MARS

SHINJI PARK

산지니

CONTENTS

A PLIM from MARS

Chapter 1

Billy's mum gave Billy a box. A lunch box. Billy went out of the house and walked towards the park. When he arrived at the park, the sun was going down. He sat by the big pond and watched the ducks playing for a while. Then he tore some pan cakes and threw them to the ducks. Suddenly a blue monster, no, a blue creature popped up from the pond. Billy started to run. He thought the blue creature was dangerous.

"Hey, Hey Boy, I will not do any harm to you. Well, Boy I haven't got enough power to beat you. I'm really small. See, Come here!"

The creature was really small. That was true. So trusting the creature, Billy sat where the blue creature was.

"W.. W.. What are you?" said Billy stepping back a bit further.

"How rude. You should say 'Who are you?' Hey? I'm

Plim. All right? Boy?" said the creature softly.

"Sorry, Is your name Plim?" Billy felt a bit more braver seeing the blue creature was teeny-weeny.

"You're very unclever boy. Plim is a name for all the creatures who look like me. For an example a Cod, that isn't a name like well, Amy, Emma, Jack or some thing. What's your name by the way?" said the Plim.

"It's Billy. What is your name, may I ask you?" asked Billy politely.

"My name is Giniel. Billy is a nice name for a little boy. You look like a good little boy then naughty you're ok. More than ok really." Giniel murmured.

The day was dark and Billy had to go home because he had promised his mum he would come home when it got dark.

"Giniel, I got to go because I promised my mum I'd come straight back home when it got dark." said Billy to the Plim.

"All right. Can you come tomorrow?" asked the Plim.

"I'll try Giniel. Bye!" Billy ran home in delight. He would be a champion finding a talking creature. But he had to keep it a secret.

The next day he went to the pond. He called "Giniel !!!"

"Is anybody out there apart from you Bill?" called a tiny voice.

"No!"

The creature popped up.

"I wondered all day if you are a thing I mean a creature which lives in ponds." asked Billy.

"Of course not, my boy. And call me Plim instead of creature if you don't mind because that sounds better. Anyway, I needed a little boy or a girl because I needed some help. So, I waited and waited for a perfect little child, You see." replied Giniel.

"Then why didn't you get some help from adults? Because they are greater and clever than little children. Well, they think they are." said Billy sitting down.

"I know that adult will spread the news round and I don't want them to. You know." said the Plim munching Billy's sandwiches busily.

"Oh, I see!" Billy knew adults were different from little children.

"Anyway I am a Plim from Mars." said Giniel taking another sandwich of Billy's.

"How can I help you?" asked Billy politely.

"I was waiting for that question, mate. You got to help me to make my spacecraft." said the Plim.

Billy was very astonished of this. How on earth was he going to make a *Spacecraft*???

"I'm sad to say this Gin, but I can't make a spacecraft. Honestly."

The Plim laughed and laughed untill Billy was angry.

"What's so funny?"

"You're, no, human being especially little child like you can't ever make a spacecraft." He shouted still laughing.

"Then how are you going to make the spacecraft then, Silly?" asked Billy getting cross.

"Don't be cross. Billy the Silly, Oupsy Daisy. I know how to make it. Don't you worry about that boy. All you need to do is get some materials I need!" said the Giniel calming down.

Billy started laughing too.

"Right, what do you need? So, I can bring it tomorrow." said Billy and added. "If possible."

The Plim seemed to be searching his red sweater.

"Here we are." Giniel said at last. He showed Billy

what looked like a mini computer.

"What I need immediately is a piece of long wood at least 1(one) meter long. I hope you can carry that secretly. If imaginable though, I don't want to make you weary. And please be careful to bring me a very sharp knife that would do for tomorrow." said Giniel looking very tired and hungry.

"Okay, Giniel. See ya!"

Billy shouted and ran. Billy could hear Giniel shouting. "Do not forget my tuna sandwiches. I'm ravenous!"

Chapter 2

When Billy arrived home, his little sister Lucy was (aged 5) packing her stuff.

"Luce, Luce, Lucy!" called Billy putting his bags down.

"What?" replied Lucy.

"Why are you packing your bag?"asked Billy furiously.

"The school holidays are coming after 3 days and we're going to visit Granny's for a week and we will come back on next Saturday." explained Lucy.

"No, I'm not going!" shouted Billy without knowing what he was doing.

"Why not, Billy? I love going to Granny's because Grandpa takes you to the beach and buys for you, whatever you want, and Grandma gives you ice creams and spider jellys and apple puddings! And remember Grandma's garden? It is beautiful and --"

"Shut up!" yelled Billy and rushed up to his room.

"Hugh..~" sighed Lucy and carried on what she was

doing. Of course, Billy's mum had heard Billy yelling at innocent girl. So she went over to Billy's room.

"Billy Becker, you'd better apologize to your sister." said Mrs Becker Calmly.

"No! You don't even know why I shouted at Lucy but you just go to Lucy's side and that's not fair, Mummy. You should know better than me!" said Billy, astonishing Mrs Becker extremely.

"Oh, for goodness sake! For heaven's sake! Are you really Billy Becker. Are you really my boy? What a disgusting behaviour!" Mrs Becker roared.

"Tell me Billy then why you've shouted to Lucy."

Billy thought for a second what to say to blame Lucy.

"Well, When I saw Lucydumbo packing her stuff, I asked her why she was doing that. And she yelled at me, so I yelled back. That's the whole tale." said Billy, trying hard to look innocent.

"Oh, So, You thought I would believe your untrue tale, Did you?" continued Mrs Becker. "Tell me why you did it please..."

So, Billy told the whole truthful tale. And he decided he would go. Because he had a quick beautiful idea in his mind.

Chapter 3

Billy arrived at the pond again in the night. He called. "Giniel, Billy Becker here. No one round."

"What is it so late, Billy? Have you got any trouble or what, Mr Becker? I need some sleep." Giniel said rather crossly.

"Well, I do have some trouble here, Giniel. Well in three days time, I am going to Cornwall." Billy began.

"Where ever is that, boy? Why are you going there? And What For?" Giniel sat on a stone with a shocked face.

"Right, Gin. Stop interrupting and liste(n)..."

Before Billy could finish the sentence off, Giniel popped into the water. Billy looked around mysteriously. There were policemen with some sort of lamp. Billy knew he was in a big trouble if he was caught by one of those policemen. He started to run as fast as his legs could carry him. As he got to the door of the park, a security was locking the door.

"Oy! You, what are you doing here so dark and you are barely 10, 7, I guess. Without a guardian!!" the security shouted angrily. The police who was chasing after Billy caught him, had a word with the security. Billy and the police made their way to the police station.

Chapter 4

Mr and Mrs Becker was called into the police station with Lucy looking messy and sleepy. And also Billy's baby brother Callum came fast asleep in his pram. While two policemen were telling Mr and Mrs Becker what was going on, Billy went away with a policeman and a policewoman. Then Billy took it very serious. He didn't actually take it serious before. He thought he was going into jail but when he was led to a room, he was relieved.

"Right, What is your name, young man?" the policewoman, Miss Dale asked.

"Billy Becker."

"Full name?"

"Billy Luke Lesley Becker." Billy replied, looking round the room. "I am Miss Dale and he is Mr Johnson. Mr Johnson is going to ask you some questions and I am going to take some notes. Don't worry. Relax. You're not going to jail!" She smiled.

Then Billy started to relax. At least he wasn't going to be in jail! Mr Johnson started asking questions.

"What were you exactly doing, Billy?"

Billy thought hard he was not going to mention about Giniel.

"I was just sitting by the pond."

"Why were you sitting by the pond in the middle of the night when there could be crazy people around?"

"I thought I would go out for a walk, Mr."

"In the middle of the night?"

"Doesn't make sense to me."

And the question went on and on. But Billy managed to not mention about Giniel.

Chapter 5

When they got home from the long dreary midnight at the police station, there were more awful events to go on for Billy. Lucy definitely didn't want to miss the actions, so she made an excuse that she was hungry. Whole Beckers family except for Callum Becker were all sitting around. There was a pause for a moment. Then Billy's dad spoke.

"Billy, it isn't very usual that you bring trouble to this family. What's the matter with you? Anything bad going on at school?"

"Nothing."

Billy just knew which question was going to come up. He decided to make something up.

"Well, I'd dreamt that there was something waiting for me by the pond." Billy said shakily.

This is quite true Billy thought.

"Billy Becker, take this serious. Don't be daft. You

seem so strange nowadays as I think about it. Your be-
havior at me, shouting at Lucy without any reason." his
mother snapped.

"He's ill." Lucy said happily.

"Lucy, it is very late. I want you to go to bed now." Mr
Becker said to Lucy firmly yawning.

Lucy had to go and she did. When she did, Billy felt a
lot better.

"Well, we're all tired and we need to sleep. This
wasn't a good experience for you at the age of 6. So, I
want you forget about it all. But I do want you to remember not to do it ever again."

Billy's dad said yawning for third time.

"Promise?" He asked smiling.

"Promise with all my heart." Billy promised so glad.
This night would be over.

Chapter 6

After school Billy ran to the pond. He checked no one was around and called Giniel.

"Billy calling. No one around."

Giniel popped up.

"Oh, oh Bill, are you all right?" Plim asked.

"I'm fine." Billy replied.

"Good for you mate! I was so worried about you! Carry on what you were saying from yesterday. You're going to 'Cornbrick' or something." Giniel asked happily seeing the sandwiches laid in front of him.

"Oh yes! I'm going to Cornwall for a week. I and my family are going to Cornwall to visit our grandparents. Cornwall is a town in South of England. It's very near the sea as far as I know." he said collecting all the information he could think of.

"So, does that mean I won't be able to see you for a week and so a week wasted. And of course, no more tuna sandwiches." he said munching the leftover tuna.

"Yeah, but I had an idea. It maybe very good one. What if you come with me? It wouldn't be very comfy for you because you won't be able to talk or move when I don't want you to." Billy explained.

"Yeah. If I go, I could be with you and eat proper foods. But what's the point? I can't even move! Food will be fine. I can eat some bits of bread those men give to ducks." said Giniel.

"I haven't finished my speech, yet. My grandad is superb at making stuff. I could ask him to make out shapes you need. I could ask him to put them together. And he could complete the spacecraft. That's my point. Oh no! Late for tea again! Think about it! See ya!" and Billy ran as fast as he could.

Chapter 7

"Billy Becker! You're late for tea again! No more of your daft excuses. You are late again and no tea and you're reported to Dad. Clear?" His mum said crossly.

"Yes mum. It is crystal clear." Billy said cheerily.

"Have you packed your suitcase?"

"Yes, mum."

"Good. I forgot to tell you but we're going to Cornwall tomorrow night."

So, Billy needed to think of another plan. He had planned everything for the Saturday morning but if they were leaving at Friday he will need another plan. He was going to say he was going out for a walk on Saturday. But he couldn't go out for a walk at night, that didn't make sense.

Billy could go and get Giniel from the park after school on Friday. But if he did, he was going to be late for tea. So he needed to get Giniel today or there won't be any other way. He didn't want to go out in the middle of the night. The only chance Billy thought is now. There was another problem. He couldn't just go out saying 'I'm going to the park.' He was sure his mother would ask a million questions. The only way was to lie. Billy didn't want to do it but he had to.

"Mum, I made a friend with this boy in reception and his house is near the park by the big tree. Can I go round there, please? I'll come home before dinner, promise." Billy begged in a way he never had done it before. Mrs Becker noticed it too and was astonished, but she stayed quiet and said yes. Billy ran out of the house delighted towards the park.

When he arrived at the pond, he called,

"Giniel, Billy here, No one." Billy whispered quickly so he could get home before it was too dark.

"Hello! What?" said Giniel kindly but not looking so happy woken up by Billy in his nap.

"Have you decided about Cornwall stuff? Because if you haven't you need to decide now." Billy said breathlessly.

"I have. I thought about it for ages. I hate being uncomfy. Not being able to speak or move when I want to! That's not my sort of thing. But I've decided for my spacecraft I'm going!"

"Yeah!" shouted Billy not too loudly.

Billy hurriedly put Giniel into his pocket.

"You can speak when I put my hands in my pocket, but you can't when I haven't got my hands in my pocket. And you can't wriggle. We got to careful, right? This is human world, Crystal Clear?"

"Uh huh."

"Good. Let's go!"

Chapter 8

When Billy got home, he had his dinner and was sent straight to bed.

The next morning came and Billy washed and he knew there was something not usual he knew but forgot about. He's going to Cornwall. It wasn't that! That was usual. Plim! Giniel! He was still in his jumper. He dried his face and ran back to his room. He shaked Giniel softly and gently.

"Giniel ! Giniel ! wake up, it's morning." Billy whispered silently.

Giniel opened one eye and the other.

"Where are you going to be while I'm gone? You could stay at home but it's not safe. Mum could sneak in and attack, Callum could crawl in and attack. Lucy comes home early than me so there is possibility she could barge in and attack." Billy whispered and his voice rose as he spoke about Lucy. Although Billy's voice wasn't that loud. Callum wake up and began to cry. Mum came up bitterly. Mum barged in. Billy desperately put Giniel in his schoolbag and smiled.

"Don't you dare wake Callum again. You will be late for school. Hurry up. Your breakfast is ready."

Mrs Becker said sharply and hurried out. Billy fished Giniel out of his school bag.

"Have you got a pond in your garden? I'll stay in there if you give me some tuna sandwiches." Giniel said.

"You're a genius. I'll give you three sandwiches."

Billy got dressed and went down. Billy safely squashed in his shirt pocket.

Billy sneaked to the garden pond and put Giniel in there with promised sandwiches and whispered "See you."

Chapter 9

At school Billy couldn't concentrate. Nothing Miss Dent said came into his head. At lunch time, Billy had to starve. Mrs Becker usually gave Billy 2, but before he had met Giniel, he insisted 1 sandwich. But now he begged his mum for three. Mrs Becker would have been no happier to give Billy three. Billy, now had no sandwiches because he had given all of his sandwiches to Giniel. He said to himself that he will survive with a drink, one bag of crisps and an apple.

When school was over, he was delighted. No school for two weeks! Billy didn't really enjoy school as a 6 year old child. Obviously because he didn't have friends. The friend in reception, Billy said to his mum was fake. He had no friend in his school. It was no wonder that he was over the moon when holiday came! Billy ran home saying 'goodbye' to his school.

Chapter 10

"Am I late for tea again mum?" Billy asked.

"No." she replied smiling.

"Good." he said dumping his school bag on the floor and saying 'Good bye for a week'.

"I'm going out to the garden!" he yelled.

At the same time Lucy came in when Billy called 'Giniel'.

Quick and sharpish he popped Giniel down and hissed "Down."

"Lucy! What are you doing here?" he said with his cheeks bright red. His cheeks became bright red if he was embarrassed or if pressure was on.

"Who's Gini? Anyway what are you doing here as well?" Lucy asked suspiciously.

"Who's Gini?" Billy asked, trying to sound normal. He might have sounded normal but he knew he didn't look normal.

"You said Gini when I entered this garden."

Lucy muttered, not taking her eyes off Billy.

"What are you doing? You said you never ever liked this garden." Lucy said.

"Well, I changed my mind. I'm watching the fishes. Get lost Luce! You're got nothing to do in this garden." Billy shouted. The pressure that he was getting angry and losing temper wasn't on Billy anymore.

It was the temper when he met Giniel. Nobody could blame the Plim.

"Well, I'm watching the fish too." Lucy was now well used to the new temper Billy made friends with.

"No, Lucy Becker! Go away, before I have to tell you again!" This time Billy's voice was so fierce that it threatened poor Lucy and made her go into the house.

Billy smiled. "You can speak, Gini" he ordered Giniel in a small. "Ow, what did you press me into the water for, ow–ow–ow~~~~h! Urgh!" Giniel yelled with all his voice, but it only sounded like normal people's voice to Billy. But it was a massive yell to the fishes and the plim. But it was louder than Billy thought. His mum had heard.

"What was that, dear?" Mrs Becker came rushing just in case it was a emergency.

"Oh, um. . . . " Billy had to think of an excuse quickly. "Just a play!" he smiled with a fake smile.

"A play? I never thought you liked plays. I've got a book full of plays you know. I loved plays. Come in and have a tea and go to the bed. We'll have to leave at 4 o'clock sharpish to catch the train at 5."

Billy did as he was told.

Chapter 11

"Billy, dear! Wake up!" his mother hissed very quietly. 'Probably trying not to wake Callum up again because he is a pain', Billy thought. He was just getting out of the bed when something wriggled in his sweater.

"Huh?" Billy said astonished. His memory wasn't good enough. It was Giniel in his pocket!

Who else could it be? Billy heard a familiar groan he'd heard several times before, Giniel!!

"Gini! Giniel! Wake up and don't make a noise. It's not a usual morning with Callum yelling! You could be heard even if it was a whisper!" Billy said cautiously. He had to be careful or else. Or else there would be trouble. Trouble laid out just for Billy.

"Why is it so unusual morning? I've never had un-usual mornings." he whispered. Billy could hardly hear him but he caught a few words.

Giniel opened his eyes.

"Or unusual midnight. What did you wake me up for an a such a chilly mor... MIDNIGHT!" He said or yelled a bit.

"We're going to Cornwall! Remember?" Billy said yawning for the hundredth time.

"Oh yeah, Cropbrick!" Giniel remembered and gave Billy half yawn and half smile.

Billy got dressed in a Pokemon Tee shirt and some old jeans. All his recent clothes were packed in a large trunk and suitcases.

"Giniel, from now on you MUST NOT, speak out of order. If you are so desperate, just give me a tap. Don't wrig...."

"That's the hundredth time you told me, Billy Boy! Don't be so grown up-ish. Your lecture is especially boring than other people's." Giniel moaned.

"That's how important it is. OK. Hop on Going down for breakfast. Be careful you don't wrig..." Billy stopped and didn't say anything else.

Chapter 12

On the train it was hot. Billy was sweating and he was squashed as well. There were three bags next to Billy. And Lucy was sitting beside the three bags. His mum and dad had two enormous bags between them but they didn't seem to be hot or squashed. On the carriage there were only the Beckers. They were all quiet.

" ♬ ♪ DuhDuh Old Macdonald had a farm EiEiO ♫ ♪ " Suddenly from now here came the singing.

"Shut up Gini." Billy whispered very quietly.

Unfortunately Lucy heard it. But luckily mum and dad were asleep.

"What was that? or Who was that?" Lucy spoke.

"That was me, singing." Billy said pulling out a innocent expression.

"Wasn't Your mouth was closed all right? What is it?"

Billy knew Lucy would never stop asking. So he made Lucy swear that she won't tell anybody.

"I'll only tell you if you promise."

"Promise."

"Copy me." Billy said, thinking again if this was a good idea.

"I'll never ever tell anybody my brother's secret." Billy whispered.

"I'll NEVER EVER tell anyone my brother's secret." Lucy copied.

"If I ever do," Billy continued. "I'll... Walk in fire and hope to die." Billy finished.

"If I ever do, I'll hope to die." Lucy said.

"And walk in fire." Billy added.

"Yeah... Walk in fire." Lucy copied.

"Plus, I'll be my brother's slave forever and ever."

"Plus, I'll be my brother's slave forever and ever."

Lucy was yawning, she thought she'd rather not know the secret than have to copy Billy's words, word by word.

"Whatever happens, no matter What..."

Billy continued ignoring Lucy's bored face.

"Whatever happens, no matter... yawn What... And I swear and promise not to tell AnyBody."

Lucy added her extra bit, for she knew Billy would

make her say that.

"Exactly."

Chapter 13

"You haven't told me your secret yet! What is it? I swore and promised. I promised and swore. But you haven't told me yet."

Lucy complained to her brother.

They were now in Cornwall or Corpbrick as Giniel called it. And Lucy still hadn't discovered Billy's secret.

"Later."

After dinner at their grand parent's house, Billy and Lucy ran to their granddad's shed. Billy's pocket was wriggling like mad. The shed door opened creaking. Lucy went in, then Billy.

"Giniel, You can talk, dance, wriggle, come out. And if you must you can sing Old Macdonald had a farm." Billy said sitting down on the tool box.

"Giniel, Gini and Gin. Very familiar or too familiar. Come on who ever you are Giniel!"

Billy was glad that his sister liked Giniel from the

beginning. He shouldn't have. The first sound Billy was expecting was a 'WOW'.

A big one but instead he heard.

"Aaaaaaaaaaaaaaaaaargh-Argh!"

That was Lucy. A ginormous scream rather than big WOW!

"Who're you? Don't come near! Nonononono, don't touch. First things first. Who are you?" Lucy managed to say panting.

"Don't come near! Nonono! Don't touch. First things first. Who are you? Pant pant pant." Giniel began mimicking the way. Billy had never seen before. When he saw round and surprised eyes, he realised what he had done, he said.

"Sor-ry. Really Really, Sor-ry about that a human can get nasty when someone is hungry, tired, thirsty and uncomfortable. And jealous." Giniel muttered.

"Rather alien than human, maybe." Lucy murmured recovering.

"Why jealous?" Billy asked curiously.

"Why jealous? Wouldn't you be jealous staring at people who moved around freely talked when they had to or wanted. Eating, drinking. You didn't give me a crumb or a drop, a drop of water." The little creature shouted furiously.

"Sor-ry! I didn't realise you would be hungry or thirsty." It was Billy's turn to apologize.

"That's your problem." he muttered bitterly.

"I better get some food and some drink for you. You have a gossip." Billy said.

"A Bossip? What's a Bossip? Is it when somebody bosses somebody about? or did you say Dozzip? Is that when you doze?" Giniel said.

Lucy and Billy laughed.

"No, You silly fool. I said gossip. That's when you chat about stuff, things and so-so!"

Billy told Giniel.

"Chat? Oooh! Cheat. What did you mean? Me and Luce have a cheat? Cheat? I see what you mean. Cheat to each other." Giniel nodded as if he understood.

"Chat means talking about news and stuff." Lucy explained.

"Is there something wrong with your ears?" Billy said giggling.

"No! Young Man, don't you make fun out of me! I'm from the universe. And plus, I don't use your language,

I use the my own language Marsian! It's completely strange words like like you listening to African!" he shouted crossly.

"Wow, Wow, Wow! You're from Mars. you can speak Marsian? Teach me a word, please." Lucy begged.

"Me too, Come on Gin! Please~" Billy begged too.

"All right then. I'll teach you Hi or Hello. Chiparusilay!" Giniel yelled!

"Ciposi blah leee!" Billy tried.

"Chi Pa rusay!" Lucy cried.

"Close, Chiparusilay!"

Lucy tried once again.

"Chiparusiiilay!"

"Yes! You are getting there! Chiparusilay not Chiliii-paruusiii~llay."

Giniel cried in excitement.

"Chiparusilay!" Lucy yelled.

"Chiparusilay!" Billy shouted.

Then, their granddad came in. Billy grabbed Giniel desperately and hid him in his pocket.

"What are you doing?" Granddad asked.

"We are playing Wizards." Billy said giving him a fake smile.

"And witches." Lucy added.

"Oh, right." Billy and Lucy's granddad gave them a nod. "I'll see you later!"

Before he could get out of the small shed, Billy spoke.

"Grandpa. I was just wondering if you could make a spaceship with wood?"

"Oh you little Pumpkin! You are interested in wood-work!" Granddad cried.

Billy's granddad called Billy Pumpkin for strange reasons.

Was it because his face was like a pumpkin? Or Was it because he thought Billy enjoyed Halloweens?

"Yes! I love em!" Billy lied. " Can you make it now?"

"Certainly! Coming to watch?" And Billy's granddad walked towards his workshop.

"I didn't know you were interested in wood works. Well, I'm not, so I'm going in." Lucy muttered.

"I'm not that interested either." Billy murmured.

Lucy stopped walking and turned round.

"But." Lucy started. Billy started to explain that Giniel needed a spaceship to get back to his house, Mars.

Lucy nodded uncertainly.

"I'm coming." she said finally.

"C'mon then!" Billy yelled.

Billy and Lucy ran after their granddad. Granddad had already started working. He was sitting down on a chair concentrating and measuring.

Lucy sat down on a chair next to him. Billy squeezed on the same chair next to Lucy.

"You can sit on my handmade half-finished bench, Billy boy!" Granddad said calmly.

" ♬ Where have ye been all day, Bil-ly boy, Bil-ly Boy? Where have ye been all the day, me Bil-ly boy? I've been wal-kin all day~ With me char-min Nancy Grey~ ♪ ♪ And me Nan-cy kit-tl'd me fan-cy Oh me char-min Bil-ly Boy ♪ ♬ " Lucy sang in a quiet voice so Granddad couldn't hear.

"Oh shut up Lucy." Billy whispered fiercely but he didn't look too cross.

Later, Billy and Lucy were getting bored. Their granddad had said that it was going to be finished in half an hour. When he saw that they were bored. And he gave each of them a space piece of wood and a blunt knife each. Billy made himself holding a card which said,

BILLY N
GINI frends
FOREVE*R

Lucy drew an alien with a t-shirt that said L U C Y on
it. By the time both of them had finished, granddad was
painting Billy's spacecraft. By the time their granddad
had completed the spaceship, Lucy and Billy were very
tired because it was past their bedtimes. Billy and Lucy
were sent straight to bed.

Billy and Lucy shared a room when they were in
Cornwall. It was a nice big room. On one side of the
room there was a full sized proper bed and on the other
side there was a camp bed. Billy quickly chose the full
sized bed.

"I sleep here." Billy yelled.

"No! That's not fair." Lucy cried.

"It is. I've got to sleep with Giniel, remember? I'll
need more room." Billy hissed.

"Oh yeah!" Lucy muttered as if it wasn't true.

"Granddad! GRANDDAD!" Billy yelled.

"Yes, my Pumpkin?" Granddad shouted.

"Can you bring my spaceship here? I want it in my

room." Billy said.

"Coming." said Granddad. "There you go."

"Thanks, granddad."

He switched the light off. Billy lit his lamp.

"Giniel! I've got a great idea! Wake up! Billy whispered, desperate to show his little friend about his good news.

"Yes Bill? Any sign of food. I thought you were going to give me something to eat?" Giniel said tiredly.

"Oh, I forgot. Sorry. I've got some biscuits."

He took out two digestive ones and gave them to him.

"Gin, never mind about food now. I've got some great news for you."

"And what's that?" Giniel snapped.

"The spaceship! Billy's got it! Our granddad made it for us. Look! It's over there!" Lucy spoke excitedly.

"Woo hoo! Celebrations Woo hoo! Congratulations Wee hee! La La La li la la la la la li lalala!" the plim screamed.

"La La La la la li la li li li Boom bam boom wee hee woo hoo wee hee, I'm going back home!"

Giniel carried on.

"Calm down, if Callum wakes up, we are in a big trouble. How is it going to fly, though? It's only made out of wood." Billy asked. But nobody was listening. Lucy was fast asleep and Giniel was snoring. He decided to ask him next morning. And he put off the lamp and went to bed.

Chapter 14

"Billy, Lu-cy, Wake up!" It was their grandma.

"Grandma, Grandma!" Lucy yelled.

"Good morning!" Lucy finished off. She was going to tell her about Giniel, and everything about him. But then she remembered her promises.

"Good morning madam. Could we have breakfast in bed, madam? We promise we won't make a mess. Go on Madam! Go on granny!"

Billy begged.

"Oh, all right then. I'll bring it up in a minute." Grandma went out of the room then she came back up with two trays.

"There you go, my dears. See you later."

"Bye Granny."

"Good morning to you again madam!"

Checking their grandma was out of the room, Billy wake Giniel up.

"Giniel! Waky waky! WAKE UP!" Billy yelled.

"a a a a! Waaargh!" came Callum's screaming.

"Uh oh, Billy! You'd better hide!"

Billy did. But it was unnecessary because no one came in.

"Giniel!" that was Billy whispering.

"Yes, BILLY!" Giniel yelled, irritated people calling his name over and over again.

"WHAT!"

"About the spacecraft."

"Ah, Sorry about the shoutings. You were asking me how to fly it. No worries. I've got the engine here that will start it. Where's the spacecraft? Wow! That's mine!" Giniel was jumping up and down.

"I'm working now!"

Billy and Lucy decided to watch Giniel working while eating their breakfasts. Giniel pulled out a red box. He opened it very carefully indeed. He placed it inside the spaceship.

"I'm off bye bye maybe see you someti--" Giniel was interrupted.

"Wait!" Lucy cried. "We've got some things for you. Here, this is me with Lucy on it. So you'll remember me."

"Me too." Billy handed Giniel his present.

"Please pardon my rudeness. Billy boy, thanks for EVERYTHING. I'll always remember you two. Thank you very very very much. I'll visit you sometime and send you messages in here. I'll contact you with this." He handed Lucy and Billy red mini computer. "You just open this and my message will be there. If you want to write to me, you press this blue button and say it out loud. Remember to begin with, 'Dear Giniel'. Goodbye and thank you again."

"Thanks Gin. I'll miss you. Bye!"

Lucy mumbled something but no one heard it.

Giniel waved a final wave to Lucy and Billy and flew away. Billy watched his friend flying away. He felt sad but he felt happy that his friend was happy. He wrote in his mini-computer.

Dear GINIEL

YOU ARE My friend forever I ♡ U !

FROM BILLY AND LUCY.

P.S ARE YOU IN MARS YET?

Jessica's Holiday

SCENE ONE

Jessica woke up on a fine Sunday morning. All her
family seemed to be up. She got dressed very quickly.
After that she washed and went down.
Everybody was having breakfast.

Mum	What do you want for breakfast, Jessica?
Jessica	Can I have some cereal please?
Mum	Yep. (going out of the stage)
Grace	Are you excited? I am so excited I could skip around with a fancy dress on. (excitedly and happily)
Jessica	What are you so excited about?
Grace	What!!! Oh, Gosh! Jessy doesn't even remember! (spits out cornflakes)
Mum	Don't you really remember? (enters the room surprised with cereal)
Jessica	Remember what? Are we getting our Sats

	results today?
Grace	No! It's Sunday. Guess!
Jessica	It's your birthday tomorrow?
Grace	No, that was ages ago.
Jessica	Christmas! Easter! (jumping up and down)
Grace	No! It's Spring. Easter is not far away but wrong!
Jessica	Um... Er... I know! Oh, I forgot. Yeah! We're going on holiday tomorrow to Wales!
Grace	Correct! Well done, Jessy! Excellent. (tiredly)

SCENE TWO

Mum	You ready, Grace and Jessica? (shouting)
Grace	Yep!
Jessica	Coming. (coming down the stairs with bangs as the suitcase come down)
Mum	We haven't got much time, you know! (shouting)
Grace	On my way, mother! (coming down with thuds and bangs)

Mum	Right come on, to the station. Check you've got all your things.
Grace	Yep.
Jessica	Yes.
Mum	Let's go.

All three of them got to the station and got into their train. The train started and it went slowly then very fast.

In the train.

Jessica	Mum, I'm hungry. (clutching her tummy)
Mum	Jessica, it isn't even lunchtime. (not paying much attention)
Jessica	We didn't have proper breakfast. (winging)
Mum	Oh yes we did.
Jessica	Can I have a bag of crisps then please?
Grace	How much longer do we have to go? I can't wait to arrive in Wales! (crossing her arms lying back)
Mum	Half an hour later we will be there.
Jessica	Can I?
Mum	Jessica, stop pestering and no!

Half an hour later they got to Wales.

Jessica	Mum, where we staying?
Grace	At a hotel, of course.
Jessica	I meant which hotel. (crossers her arms)
Mum	I don't know. But I know where it is. We have got a taxi booked.
Jessica	Where's the hotel near, mum?
Mum	Beach. We are going to be playing there for whole week. (smiles)
Grace	Hurrah! I do love swimming. I can swim really well. Can you, Jess? (smiling and beaming towards Jessica)
Jessica	Shurrup.
Mum	Jessica!
Jessica	But Grace's teasing me because I can't swim very well.
Mum	Here's the taxi.

The taxi comes and all three of them scurry into the seats. Jessica sat at the front, Grace and mum at the back.

Taxi driver	Are you lot Linda, Grace and Jessica Ellis?
Grace	Yep.
Taxi driver	Heading for the beach?
Jessica	Uh-Huh!
Taxi driver	Great! Here we go! (He turns on the music and he drives off)

SCENE THREE

Mum, Grace and Jessica arrive at the hotel. Mum and Grace start unpacking from their heavy suitcases.

Grace	I'm so looking forward to the next day. (she yawns) Hope it's sunny.
Jessica	I don't understand why you guys are unpacking. We're going to be going home in a week. This isn't home.
Grace	A week it seven days and that's long, Jess.
Mum	Jessy, don't start all the winges, will you?
Jessica	Just saying. Mum, have you bought my swimming costume?
Mum	Yes.

Jessica	My body is so stiff. I can't move. Ah, Ow ow.
Grace	Shurrup Jessica. You're not here to winge. Holiday is a time when you relax not winge.
Jessica	Wasn't talking to you. (under her breath) By the way, every one, I'm sleeping by the window.
Grace	You're not! I am!!
Jessica	No!
Mum	I am.
Grace	Then I'm in the middle.
Jessica	No, You can't, because I am.
Mum	Jessy, Grace was there first.
Grace	Yeah!
Jessica	But I was on the bed by window first.

Everybody went to bed because they were so tired.

SCENE FOUR

Grace	Wake up, Jessy!
Jessica	No, get out! How many times did I tell you

	to stop coming into my room?
Grace	Oh no! I don't have to tell you again do I? (Jessica wakes up)
Jessica	Huh? Where are we? Where's mum?
Grace	Jessica Ellis! You're so stupid.
Jessica	Where are we, Grace? We kidnapped.
Grace	Ergh... No! We're in Wales remember? (sighing)
Jessica	Oh yeah. I remember.
Grace	It was only yesterday. You can't even remember that?
Jessica	Not really where's mum anyway? (irritated)
Grace	She's having breakfast. Let's go. I'm hungry.
Jessica	Me too.

Jessica and Grace go down to breakfast room. They find their mum's table, number fifteen and sit down.

Grace	Are the foods nice?
Mum	They are lovely. You've got to order what you want if you're having hot food.

Cornflakes, toasts are there.

Grace	Ok, Mum call a waiter or waitress for me.
Mum	Waitress!

Jessica leaves the table towards toasts.

Waitress	Can I help you?
Grace	Could I have bacon and scrambled egg please.
Waitress	Anything else?
Grace	Cold drink?
Waitress	All sort of drinks are over there.
Grace	Thank you.
Waitress	I'll bring your plate in a sec.

Jessica comes back on to the table and sits down. The waitress comes back with Grace's plate. Mum gets Jessica and Grace's drinks and they start eating.

Grace	The food is really good.
Jessica	The toast is really really good.
Mum	Don't talk with your mouth full, Jessica.

When they had finished their breakfast, they went back to their room.

SCENE FIVE

Grace	Hurry up, Jess. I'm waiting. (pretending to yawn)
Jessica	I can't find my swimming costume. I'm sure I left it here last night. (searching through her clothes) Go without me, I will catch you guys later. (pointing to the door)
Grace	You don't even know the way to the entrance, dumb.
Jessica	Mum, I can't find it.
Mum	Can't find what?
Jessica	Swimming costume.
Mum	Where did you put it last night?
Jessica	On the shelf.
Grace	I'll do it. I'll find it you wait and see.
Jessica	Huh!
Grace	(slowly) Look and learn, Jessy! Here it is!
Jessica	Where on earth d-

Grace	Shurrup and come on.
Jessica	Coming.

SCENE SIX

All three of them finally went out to the beach. It was a very hot day. The sun was dazzling above hotels, beaches and people.

Grace	Come on, Jessy! Come and have a swim. Won't tease you.
Jessica	I'm hot.
Grace	The water is cool. Come on! (Jessica shooks her hood)
Mum	I'll get both of you an ice cream each if you want.
Grace	Yes, please!
Jessica	Oh yeah!
Mum	What flavour?
Jessica	Strawberry!
Grace	Chocolate!
Mum	Another flavour?

Grace	Vanilla!
Jessica	Mm.... Apple no I meant melon or Kiwi. I'd prefer Kiwi.
Grace	Urgh! Jessica likes apple, melon and Kiwi flavour. Yuck!

Mum goes to buy ice creams.

Jessica	It's actually really delicious you know. You always have chocolate and Vanilla. No wonder you're always ill, always choosing unhealthy foods. I always eat fruit.
Grace	Any way Jess, don't you want a swim? I'll teach you. (loudly)

Several people look at them and some boys snigger.

Jessica	(In whisper) I'm going to kill you Grace Ellis. (loudly) I don't need your help, thanks. I can swim fine. But I don't want to swim now.

Mum comes in with three ice creams one each for all three of them.

Grace	Mmm.. Chocolate and Vanilla. Mum's got Vanilla and Strawberry.
Jessica	I've got Kiwi and melon.
Grace	Double yuck! (pretending to be sick)
Mum	They ran out of strawberry.
Jessica	Don't matter. Yum yum. (licking the ice cream)
Grace	You're a complete weirdo.
Jessica	I love being a weirdo! (beaming)

SCENE SEVEN

A wonderful hot and bright day passed. On the fourth day of their holiday Grace woke up first as usual, then mum. (Jessica's alarm rings)

Alarm	R r r r ring Wwake uup J J J Jessy c c ca!

Jessica turns off the alarm and gets ready for breakfast.

Jessica	What's the plan today? Sea again?

	I'm quite seasick now!
Mum	We will do something different today.
Jessica	Stay in bed and rest.
Grace	No Way! Jessica Ellis! You are so ungrateful to be on holiday! You should be at school working Work! Work! Work! You ungrateful girl. (Jessica snort)
Mum	Why don't we go to the country park and have a walk there.
Grace	Naaa! I've got a superb Idea! Why don't we go to that theme park? Then to the Zoo! That waitress said the Zoo was just up the street. A tour round the city. Visit the shops. Go on!
Jessica	Yeah! We could ride those scary rides, Zoo! Talk about it. We could see zebras and tigers, r-roar! Visit Next! Get me some clothes, mum.
Mum	All right. To breakfast Room, now.

SCENE EIGHT

After breakfast they caught the bus that went to the Wales Theme Park.

Mum	A family ticket please.
Bus Driver	Here you go.
Mum	Thanks.
Jessica	Mum, Let's go up. Please let's do what I want to do for once.
Grace	No! We won't know where the theme park is, if we sit up there. We'll miss our stop to come down those stairs.

Mum sits on the back seat. Grace sits behind her. Jessica sits as far away from Grace.

Jessica	(mutters) Do you always have to disagree with me, Gracedumbo? You're old and older than me to realise that.
Bus driver	Wales Theme Park Stop!
Grace	Come on Jessica! This is the theme park stop!

Mum	Jessica Ellis! Did you hear Grace?
Jessica	(under her breath) I probably did. But I don't want to listen to her, do I?
Grace	Jessica! The bus is moving! Move it!
Jessica	Can't you see I'm moving. (whispering) 'Puss in boots'? (shouting) Coming!

Out of the bus and at the gates of the Wales Theme Park

Grace	Mum, Jessica -
Jessica	What have I done wrong, now?
Grace	Jessica said I'm a 'pusspot' because I told her to get out of the bus.
Jessica	'Puss in boots' not pots.
Grace	Whatever.
Mum	Both of you! Stop this pathetic behaviour. I'm quite sick of it, thank you. I hear once more you two quarreling over STUPID things, We go back to the hotel!
Jessica	Hurrah! And rest.
Mum	I have not finished yet. And Work.
Jessica	Oh.

They go into the Theme Park and have fun. They go to the Zoo and have a city tour and mum's favourite part going shopping.

SCENE NINE

Back in their rooms

Jessica	What day is it?
Grace	Monday.
Jessica	Tisn't.
Grace	Tis. It is. Isn't it Monday today?
Mum	It's Tuesday. And would you stop arguing? Thank you.
Grace	Mum!
Mum	What!
Grace	Can I go out and play?
Mum	I need a rest, Grace.
Grace	With Jessy.
Jessica	No! I don't want to go! It's cold! Mum, I'm a human! I need a rest. You can't make me go.
Mum	If Grace's got energy to go out and play,

you can because Grace is a human.

Jessica	She isn't. She's an alien. Anyway she can go out on her own.
Mum	Go, Jessica!
Grace	Give us some money!
Mum	Get my purse and take £2(2pounds) for each of you. And off you go.
Jessica	At least I've got some money. I'm not playing with Grace. Actually I won't even go near her, so no one will think I'm actually her sister.

Grace and Jessica, by the door

Mum	And remember! Stay together!

Jessica stamps her foot.

Jessica	That is not fair.
Grace	What shall I do with my money? I'll buy double scoop ice cream, a bottle of cola, one packet of crisps, loads of sweets and chocolates, a diary, a holiday present...

Jessica	Well, buy it then.
Grace	Come with me!
Jessica	No! I'm going to the beach and don't copy.
Grace	I'm going to the beach as well.
Jessica	Grace! you copycat.

SCENE TEN

After an ice cream or two, Jessica is a good mood.

Grace	Hey, Jessica! I know what we can do! Say we are explorers. I'm captain Grace and you're Cook Jessica.
Jessica	Noooo! I'm captain Jessica. It suits better. Cook Grace sounds a lot better than Cook Jessica, too.
Grace	Okay! We can both be captains. Captain Jessica and Captain Grace.
Jessica	Yeah, we can say that we've discovered an island and we're digging for treasure that Pirate Joanne and Joeseph has left. Captain Grace let's start digging.

Grace	You don't really have to dig. There's nothing as pirates treasures are from fairy tales. It doesn't exist in the modern world.
Jessica	Well, it exists to me.
Grace	Doesn't to me.
Jessica	Whatever just dig, Captain, G.
Grace	Yes sir, Captain, J.

After 6 or 7 minutes. Both of them are sweating.

Grace	Jessy-caaa, I'm sweating. Let's spend some money and go in.
Jessica	No, Grace! I don't want to – LOOK! Grace, Captain G, Come here!
Grace	What is it, What, What, Captain J?
Jessica	Captain Grace! Treasure.
Grace	Oh, don't be silly.
Jessica	I am not being silly, Grace. Honestly. Just come and have a look at this. It won't do any harm to you taking a peek. There's a chest!
Grace	You're so babish. You are ten--. Treasure Chest! It is really a treasure chest! Wow,

	Captain Jess! Well done!
Jessica	Thank you! Thank you! Let's dig. So we can get it out!
Grace	Yes sir!

They began working. Grace didn't mind sweating so much now.

Jessica	I think we've dug enough. Captain G. Pull~ stronger. P~u~l~l! Once more, hup! There we are. I'll open it.
Grace	Oh my word! It's real gold! We will be a billionaire!!
Jessica	Not we! It's I!! Jessica the kid billionaire, Woo hoo!
Grace	Boo Hoo, Jessica. I'll see you later.
Jessica	No! Come here. I'll share all of it. No, half of it. No, non. I mean the quarter of it. You'll still be rich.
Grace	Oh, all right, then!
Jessica	Captain G, help me carry it.
Grace	Yes, Captain Jessica.

At the hotel entrance,

Hotel manager Sorry, ladies but we don't let this dirty, rusty box in this hotel.

Jessica But it's worth it.

Grace Yeah, it's got treasure in this chest. Show her, Jess.

Jessica Look.

Hotel manager Wow. The museum has been looking for this treasure for centuries.

Hotel manager rings the museum. In a second, there are reporters everywhere all over the hotel. After a tired evening taking photos, Grace and Jessica went to bed.

Next morning

Mum Jessica, are you up?

Jessica I think I am. (Yawn)

Mum Get me a paper.

Jessica When I'm ready.

Grace I'll go.

Mum 90p(penny) here you go.

Grace	Can I get something with the spare money?
Mum	You halve the change, fairly.
Jessica	(brushing her teeth) Get me as many salt and vinegar crisps. Give me the change though.
Grace	Okay.

Grace comes back yelling.

Grace	I'm in the paper. In the front page!!
Jessica	I am, as well! I'm saying most of the things.

A bunch of people and pack of reporters knock. Grace not knowing open the door. All of them pour in. Desperate to speak to Jessica and Grace first.

Jessica	I'm a billionaire kid and famous at last!

The End

Treasure Adventure

Treasure Adventure

Crisps eater Chris was munching his crisps busily in a corner. Lovely Lilly was sitting on the bed her head in her book. Sporty Sian was jumping up and down.

Nobody was paying attention and driving me CRAZY.

"There's nothing more important thing to you than eating, is there Chris?"

I shouted crossly.

"Move it, all of you! We're going on a journey to find the treasure! Isn't that anything to you?"

The others lazily checked their trunks, making sure they had all their equipment.

"Can I just finish this?" he asked.

"No!" We all replied looking at Chris sharply.

"Oh right! All Right." Chris muttered.

I'll try and explain everything if I remember it all. Right here is the story. One day I saw this advertisement on the newspaper about treasure that a famous pirate buried in a small town called Bure. Pronunciation: Bu-rei. Sian had trouble pronouncing that.

Anyway I was eager to find it. Lilly, my best friend volunteered to do it with me. Tim, Lilly's brother was keen to come too, but I didn't let him come. He can be a pain in the neck. Chris moved into our town a month ago and he became friends with Sian. Lilly lives in the same street as Sian. She asked her. Sian said "yes". Sian was very keen to take Chris with us. But Chris didn't want to come. Lilly told me he was too busy with his chocolate muffins. But in the end Chris gave up and decided to go.

That's the story. Hang on, I've forgot to tell you some things. We decided to call ourselves 'The Fab four'. We added words in front of our names. Because we thought it would sound boring just our names, like Bella in a history book. By the way I'm Bella.

I'm Brave Bella. Obviously I'm brave. There is Lovely Lilly. Me and Sian wished Lilly's name began with a C. So she can be clever something because she is clever. But it began with a L. Sian suggested Lovelife-less Lilly for some reason. Chris suggested Lovely Lilly. I agreed with that. I think Chris fancies Lilly, honestly.   But I won't go into that now. This is a red thick book. I'm writing in. Oh, Sorry! I forgot that I didn't finish about the names.

We named Sian, sporty Sian. She loves football and she can run faster than anybody in our school. Sian decided to be Chris's friend. So she can exercise Chris because he hates running.

Finally there is Chris, Crisps eater Chris. You can re-alize why that is. And you know pretty well that Chris just LOVES crisps. Any flavour. He especially likes Bar-becue flavour.

OK. About the red thick book. It's got gold borders and it's old fashioned style-ish book. Chris's mum got it for us. Although, Chris's mum, Mrs Hazel appreciates her son eating so much, she was happier to buy Chris a book to write and draw on. Chris said she screamed and said, "Oh, Chris you chubby little thing! You've at last learnt how exciting writing is!"

Lilly put THE RECORD BOOK in a neat writing with gold gel pen. We decided to take turns to write what's going on. And I'm the first one to write on it. We're all in Chris's huge bedroom resting after our long journey. Lilly's on the bed having a little nap. Sian is lying on her bed staring at the Today's Sport magazine in her hand. Chris as usual is on the floor opening another Snicker chocolate bar and munching it. Tim is sleeping quietly next to Lilly. You'll get to know Tim later. He's Lilly's brother aged 5. Thank goodness he's asleep.

I am writing as you know. I'll start the story. I'll stop telling you what's going on now. I'll tell you more about what went on.

You ready? Here we go... Oh! Brother! I just don't know what to write. Half of me is saying. What do I write Miss Mckenny(my surname)? The other half is saying. This is suppose to be a Record Book, Miss Mckenny. It will be in history books. You don't say I don't know what to write in a history book, do you? Miss Mckenny, Get ON!

Okay, so when we were ready to go, we went in to Lilly's kitchen to pack some food(Chris's favourite part). I saw Tim watching us his brown eyes screwed up. Then he disappeared. When we packed all the foods, we all collected our stuff. We walked to the station with Chris moaning behind us.

"Right guys! This is the moment of our lives, when we'll be billionaires so ch--" I started.

"Aaargh! Watchat, Belinda, behind you!" Lilly screamed calling me Belinda. When Lilly called me Belinda she is always serious. But I don't like being called Belinda. It's such an old fashioned name. Mum says it's a BEAUTIFUL Name! And dad says it's popular. As if. If dad is telling the truth, I bet you it was popular in Medieval Times.

No thank you. I wouldn't like a name that was popular in Medieval times.

"That was the moment you could be knocked over by a van, Bella Mckenz!" Sian joked.

"Oh, Sian!" That's me. We all had a laugh. Except Chris.

"Wassup?" I asked.

"This... bbag is sssoooo hea...avy." Chris tried to tell me. I could see he was really exhausted and all.

"Oh give it here." Sian took Chris's bag and hung it on her shoulder.

"Oh good, this is the station! I wouldn't mind having a seat. I've never ever WALKed to Burdon Station with trunks before."

Lilly panted. "Give us the tickets, Bella. The train will be leaving in a min."

"Come on guys. Our train's over there it says Bure!" I yelled.

I was pretty worn out myself too. Even Sian was.

"What's your seat number, Bel? Mine's number 15." Sian said putting Chris's bag down and picking it up again.

"Urgh, this bag is heavy! What have you put in this bag, Chris Hazel, the whole fridge? I hope not." she muttered.

"I'm number 27. I'm miles away from you, Sian." I managed to say. I had a fit of giggles. You may think It's not funny at all. In fact it wasn't the words that amused me. You should have seen the expression on Sian's face!

"Me number 18." Chris replied. He was laughing his head off.

Lilly suddenly yelled. "Guys! No time to laugh! The train's moving!"

We tried our best to get ourselves and our trunks on the train. We were all sweaty when we found our seats. Sian sat next to Lilly and Chris sat opposite Sian. Next to Chris, a snoring man was sitting there. I sat miles away from my friends. I had to sit next to this girl with her blonde hair all plaited. She cleared her stuff out of the way when I came to sit. There was a dark haired boy opposite her.

"Hi." the girl said. But I didn't say anything I just smiled. I went for a little nap because I was so tired.

I woke up ten minutes later. I got that advertisement out of my bag and a plain white paper with blue biro. Somebody shook me. It was Sian.

"Wazzup?"

"Oh, Kenny Mc, Everything. It's going to be a total disaster with Tim." Sian whispered. Sian called me Kenny Mc. My surname Mckenny? Get it?

"Tim's not here, Sian. What are you talking about?"

"Wrong Kenny!" It was Lilly. Great, she was calling me Kenny too! No more Bella or Belinda.

"What ARE you talking about?" I shouted.

"We better show kenny before she erupts!" Lilly said not smiling. Was she serious? Or What? I was led to the toilet. Chris was there.

"Show Kenny, Chris." Sian ordered. And there was Tim smiling and laughing his head off.

"T I M!" I shrieked. "What on earth are YOU doing here?" I was so mad I could have punched him in the face!

"I just wanted to come with you. I want to be in Fab four as well." he replied smartly.

"No wonder Chris's bag was so heavy, Kenz. What, with Tim in it."

Sian said glaring at Tim. I was thinking about letting Tim be in the Fab four. He was such a pain!

"Tim, I will only let you be in the Fab four if you are not naughty."

I told him. The others seemed to agree with me as well.

"You promise?"

"Sure, Kenny! Can I come out of this bag now?" he asked.

"Yes, I suppose so." I replied slowly. Tim headed for the door.

"No! Tim, no." Lilly yelled.

"The door's not going to bomb, is it? I hope not." Tim wanted to know.

"No it isn't but Tim Hall, have you got a ticket? No. Hello? Duh!"

Lilly explained. Nice point.

"I'm not going to be squashed again!" Tim howled. "No way!"

"We'll make it comfy for you, Tim. We'll take some stuff out of Chris's bag. That's what I'll do. You put Chris's stuff in my bag, Kenny. I am going to rest for a while." Sian seemed so tired I did what Sian told me to do.

When I had done it, I went back to my seat and I spotted the girl reading the advertisement.

"Hey, you! That's mine!"

"Sorry. It was interesting, so I had a little look and I just started reading it. I'd love to find the treasure." She said dreamily.

"Me and my mates are going to." I told her. I hoped to see a jealous face from her but I didn't. She just said, "Are you? Very interesting."

Then she blurted out after a moment's silence. "Do you think I could help?" She seemed so keen I couldn't say no. So I said yes. She told me about Bure. She said she was going to Bure as well. I thought the train only went to Bure. But she said it didn't. It's second stop(last stop, rather) was Inverness.

"I thought everybody was going to Bure." I said.

She laughed then and said, "Bure is a tiny town. Not actually A TOWN. It's not on map or anything it's not even quarters of Burdon. Burdon's a small town by the way -"

"How do you know Burdon?"

"Me and my mates live there!"

I told her excitedly. "Do you live in Burdon?"

"Yeah, we(her family) moved in yesterday. Mum and Dad and my big sister Louise is unpacking, sorting school out and stuff. But my school's sorted. It's Hildons Juniors. Me and Michael -" She was interrupted by her brother. "Hey, Lia! Pass me some Twix bars."

Aha! She was Lia. I liked her name. Lia passed him some then she carried on. "Me and Michael are staying with our grandparents for the holidays. Mike's my brother."

"Can I call you Lia?"

"Yep. My proper name's Leanne Valley. But people call me Lia Valley. What's your name?" She asked. I hesitated I didn't know whether to give my real name or unreal surname name. I decided to give her both. "Belinda Mckenny or Bella Mckenny. But my friends call me kenny Mc. Get it my surname Mckenny? I hate my name Belinda you see."

I explained. Lia nodded and she dozed off. I decided to do a Fab six(it becomes six instead of four, including Tim and

Lia) membership card on a piece of A3 card. These are the cards.

Fab Six Membership Card	Age: Ten
Name: Bella Mckenny	Bella Mckenny is a
Nick name: Kenny Mc	member of fab six
Fab Six name : Brave Bella	*Kenny Mc. dilly*

Fab Six Membership Card	Age: Ten
Name: Lilly Hall	Lilly Hall is a
Nick name:	member of fab six
Fab Six name : Lovely Lilly	*Kenny Mc. dilly*

Fab Six Membership Card
Name: Leanne

Just as I was trying to ask Lia her surname (I couldn't remember something) Mike said "Kenny Mc! If Leanne's in the fab six, so am I! I'm her brother!" he pointed out.

"Okay, Good point. Only it won't be Fab six anymore. It'll be Fab seven!" So poor Kenny had to start all over again!

Poor Me! Here are the new ones. 10 at the bottom is my age!

FAB 7 MEMBERSHIP CARD

Name: Bella Mckenny

N. name: Kenny Mc.

Fab 7 name: Brave Bella ⑩

That one's mine. Looks whole lot better doesn't it? Michael did it all. I only wrote name and stuff. This one is Mike's.

FAB 7 MEMBERSHIP CARD

Name: Michael Valley

N. name: Mike V.

Fab 7 name: Magnificent Mike ⑫

This one's Lia's. Mike says Lia's very girly. I don't like

girly girls but I like Lia.

FAB 7 MEMBERSHIP CARD

Name: Leanne Valley

N. name: Lia

Fab 7 name: Lucky Lia ⑩

I just named Lia, Lucky Lia. Because I couldn't think of anything else!

FAB 7 MEMBERSHIP CARD

Name: Sian Terras

N. name: The Sporty Girl

Fab 7 name: Sporty Sian ⑩

FAB 7 MEMBERSHIP CARD

Name: Chris Hazel

N. name: The eater

Fab 7 name: Crisps eater Chris ⑩

FAB 7 MEMBERSHIP CARD

Name: Lilly Hall

N. name: Smart one!

Fab 7 name: Lovely Lilly ⑩

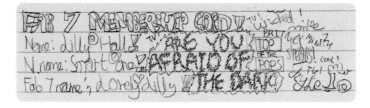

FAB 7 MEMBERSHIP CARD

Name: Tim Hall

N. name: The painful one

Fab 7 name: Tiny Tim ⑤

They all look sooo funky, don't they? (although Mike did
them all!) Anyway, back to the train. When we finished
making membership cards, we were in Bure. As Lia
said, Bure was such a small town. Only 11 people were
going to Bure out of 60 people! We were all walking
down with our bags when Chris said, "Can I let Tim out
now?" I hadn't been thinking about Tim.

"I think~~ so."

So we told Tim to hop out.

"Hello people! Who are you, two?"

Oopsy! I hadn't told the team about Lia and Mike!

"Oh! One of the Fab 7." I replied trying to sound casual.

"When did it become 7?

"When Lia and Mike joined. You don't mind do you?"

"Course not!"

"No probs!"

"Sure!"

Lilly was the one who said 'Sure.' But she didn't

sound like she meant it so I asked her.

"Anything wrong, Lils?"

"No. Nothing at all." She murmured uncertainly. "Who am I kidding? Not you. Not me. Oh kenz, where are we staying?"

"UH OH." I replied.

"Not uh oh, Kenny. It's Uh oh, Uh oh, Uh oh, Uh oh, Urgg! Why didn't we think about that? I mean it's very simple and obvious that we need a place to stay, isn't it? Well, I thought it was and it is. I mean -"

"Not to worry." Mike chipped in.

"Not to worry?" me, Lilly and Sian said together.

"What do you mean, not to worry? Yes, to worry. We'll have to sleep on streets!" Sian bellowed angrily.

"You won't be." That's Lia.

"Yes, we'll be. Probably." Lilly replied back.

"You will probably be in Dorothy Street in a house with my Grandma!!" Lia shouted.

"Oh. Good work I put Lia and Mike in the club!" I said.

"Wait, you live in Dorothy street? Where is that? Is it near here?" Lilly is always thinking about one thing.

"Yeah it's near here. Follow me." Mike spoke.

When we arrived there, Lia's grandma and grandpa

welcomed us.

"You guests, I have a spare room for you. Lia and Mike you can sleep in the small room."

"Grandpa, can these three boys sleep in the small room and us four girls in the guest room?" Lia asked.

"Do what you wish, dear. Let's have tea and you lot can go to bed early."

We ate tea. It was delicious! Especially the apple pie and raspberry pie. After our tea, we watched TV for a bit and went to sleep. In the guest room, there was one bed. Lilly and Lia slept on the bed. So me and Sian had to sleep on the floor.

Now it's Chris's turn to write.

Hi, I'm Chris. I hate writing but I have to write. In the small room Mike, Tim and I squashed on the single bed. It was so uncomfortable. I slept on the floor. The next morning I hoped there would be cheese crust pizza, a barbecue hamburger. They are my favorite food. My favorite snack is -. Kenny is shouting at me to get on with the story. Well I'd better before Kenny erupts. Well after breakfast (Shhh... The

breakfast wasn't pizzas and stuff but delicious toast)
We went to this place where the newspaper thought
the treasure was. Mike's gran told us there's only 66
people living in Bure. And Bure is so small that they
call like parts of Bure west of Bure or East of Bure
and things like that. We heard a lot of things about
Bure. Some of them helped us. The place we had to go
was West-north of Bure. We walked there. Where we
were staying was in the central of Bure but little bit
of central towards Western Bure. When we got to the
West-north of Bure, we were so surprised because we
couldn't imagine a treasure in a city like London. West-
north Bure was no different to London.
"I'm not really sure about treasures being in here."
Kenny spoke.
"Nor do I. Where is the advert? Let's read it. There
might be something. Oh, here, 'People say it will be
somewhere near Bure country park or in the Bure
country park'." It was Lilly. Lilly always sorts things
out. She knows everything. Good work. But there
wasn't any information about Bure country park. So
we went into the shop to ask.

Lilly's turn to write.

Lilly writing!
"Uh hello! We are Fab 7. Do you know where Bure country park is?" Lia asked in a sweet voice.
"Bure country park? Sorry I've never heard it."
That was the most disappointing speech that day. Things really didn't go right that day. We visited another shop.
I asked, "Hello! We are the Fab 7 and do you know where Bure country park is?"
The man smiled. And spoke.
"Hi, fab 7s. The country park is in the South Bure. It's very far for you guys to walk. You better catch a bus or a taxi."
"Thank you for the information." I said. I thought there would be no way but choose to go South Bure but Kenny's idea was different.
"I don't think we should try to finish this today. Let's go home and get some information about South of Bure. And if the country Park is there. That man could be wrong."
So we did go home. We asked Lia's grand parents for some information. But they said they didn't know a lot about Southern Bure because they had never been there.

We didn't think there will be anything about Bure on the internet. And we were right. Nothing about Bure. We didn't know what to do then. Lia asked their grandparents if they knew a person that knew some useful information about Southern Bure. They said they will look for a person. Lia's grandma told us to play in the garden. So we played all afternoon. When we were having supper, Lia's grandpa told us he found a brilliant person. He was a Bure tourist guide and knew a lot about Bure. So, we decided to visit him tomorrow. So the next day went to where he lived. He gave us some orange juice.

Lia's turn to write.

Sweet Orange juice! Sweet Lia!

The orange juice was so sweet! Just sweet like me! Aren't I?
~"Hello Lia? You aren't suppose to write about yourself! Get on!"~
Okay!! That was Kenny. Okay, So um... let's start.
After having a breakfast, Fab seven went to the Bure tourist guide. He was Mr. Stockwood. I knew him.
He lived just the next street, Queen's Pleasure

street. We decided me(Lia), Lilly and Sian go to
the Mr. Stock's house. Michael, Kenny, Tim and
Chris go to the Bure Library. They decided to get
some information from books. And they asked to the
people where is near library.

Me, Lilly and Sian went to Mr. Stock's. He
welcomed us. He told us a lot about Southern Bure.
This is the notebook Lilly noted what Mr. Stock
said;

Lilly's

> There is a tourist centre → Happy street
> There is a country park in Southern Bure
> It's in Johnson saint's street
> You should take a bus

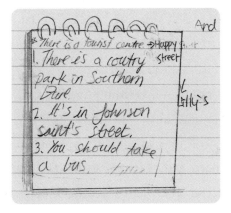

And this is Kenny's notebook.

> There is a country park (10 people)
> No (2 people)
> Don't know (5 people)
> It's in Merrilyn Street
> There is a shuttle bus or train
> (Bella Mckenny)

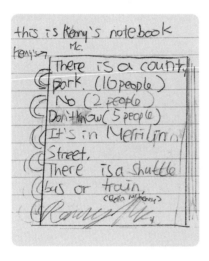

There are some different information.
We heard the country park was in Johnson saint's
street. But Kenny said in a book there was some
information about Bure and it said Merrilyn Street.
Lilly said, "First, we will go to Southern Bure.

We'll go to Johnson saint's street. And if it isn't there, we go to Merrilyn Street." We agreed. We rested for the rest of the day. I had to sleep on the floor this time with Kenny. Sian and Lilly slept on the bed. The next morning we were going to go to Southern Bure. But we decided to rest.

Mike's turn to write.

I am Mike.

It was Chris who suggested to rest. And when Chris said it, Tim was shouting, jumping up and down to rest. So most

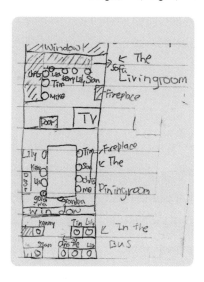

of us agreed except Sian and Kenny. They moaned when everyone agreed, but they decided to rest and play today.

I, Chris and Tim played computer games, (We had to do some stupid babish games for Tim) Sian and Kenny played football in the garden. And Lia and Lilly went shopping to Bure Central Shopping center and listened to music. It was so relaxed day, since we came to Bure. And we decided to stay up all night watching comedy videos. But we slept with the video on in the living room.

So the next morning all of us woke up late. Our grandpa and grandma were having breakfast when I woke up! It was 10:30 when all of us woke up. So we caught a shuttle bus to Southern Bure at 12 o'clock. In the bus I sat between Lia and Chris. I was so squashed and hot. I swapped seats with Chris because I thought it would be better at the end. When we arrived, we got something to eat first. Because it was lunch time when we got there. After our snacks we tried to find Johnson saint's street.

Sian's turn to write.

Hi, I'm Sian. I am too busy.
So if you're curious about more of this story, you'll have to wait a very long time. I'll tell you the rest of the story next time. Maybe you should fill the end of this story with your imagination? It's gonna be great thing!
Good bye!

SHINJI'S DUDA BOOK

: Shinji Park's PLAY BOOK AND STORY. KEEP OUT!

1. school happening
2. university, life, job
   – Lucy's life
3. you have a diary? I have chicky!!!

With thanks to Mr. Brooks who gave me the idea
and thanks to mum who told me how to write plays.
And also thanks to year 6 for being there to be my
characters.
<Also Gareth(year 6) and Mr. Birks, Miss Cross.>

school happening

character
(Everyone who comes out is a fictional character)

Alex Thorpe	**Joe Watson**
Amy Plant	Lucie Blakeman
Andrew Hall	**Luke Hardern**
Ashley Tatton	Oliver Bateman
Becky W	Oliver Drew
Callum Kerr	Oliver Sutton
Callum Morris	Poppy Holland
Chelsie Hill	**Rebecca Ward**
Daniel Pegg	Rosie Shelton
Emily Dixon	**Shinji Park**
Emily Jefferey	Terry Chloesy
Emily Watley	**Mr. Birks**
Gareth Pen	**Mr. Eves**
Goerge Hunt	Mrs. Forst
Joe Sullivan	Police 1, 2

scene One

At St. John's school, it is playtime. Rebecca Ward
arrives to school.

Shinji Park and Amy are there already.

Rebecca   Hiya!

Amy   I wonder why you're looking so happy,
               Rebecca.

Rebecca   Why?

Shinji   No sign of Miss Cross yet she should be
               here by now, if she's teaching us. So you
               know what this means?

Amy, Rebecca, Shinji   We've got Mr. Eves.

Rebecca   I wonder why I was looking so happy.

Somebody behind Rebecca takes off her hat.

Rebecca   Hey, you, Gareth! I saw that give it here,

now or else!

Gareth	What are you on about? This hat is mine. I've had it for years.
Shinji	If you don't give it back now, we'll report to Mr. Birks. We will.
Amy	You might get expelled.

Gareth throws the hat back to Rebecca.

Rebecca	Thank you.

The bell rings and everybody lines up.

scene Two

Oliver Drew   Who's teaching us today? Whoever it is, they are late.

Poppy Holland   It's him. And it's... Mr. Eves, ta-ra!

Lucie Blakeman   It isn't funny that we've got Mr. Eves today.

Terry Chloesy   Yeah, he's horrible.

The door opens and Mr. Eves enters the classroom.

Mr. Eves   Whoever started the conversation, please shut up. Miss Cross is poorly and I'll be here for probably two weeks. If you are not happy with that, please go to Mr. Birks.

Lucie.B   (whispers to Oliver Bateman) Do you think he has heard me and Terry?

Oliver.B   He's heard the whole conversation. He

said when he entered the classroom, stop the conversation.

Rosie Shelton	And he knows that we don't like him, remember he said, if you are not happy with that, please go to Mr. Birks.
Shinji	Nobody likes him.
Rosie.S	But he heard Terry say, 'he's horrible'.
Shinji	Whatever.

Luke Hardern and Joe Watson join in.

Luke.H	Look, you four. On Mr. Eves' suitcase.
Shinji	That's a bag and a purse. What's wrong about that? I don't find anything wrong with that.
Joe.W	You don't realise whose it is.
Lucie	It's Mr. Eves'.
Luke.H	It isn't.
Ashley Tatton	Ah! That bag is Callum Morris's.
Emily Watley	And the purse is–Mine!
Joe.W	Yes, that's what we noticed.

More people round them join in to the conversation.

Callum Kerr	That's not yours, Emily.
Emily.W	It is.
Emily Jefferey	It is, Callum. Look it says there, Emily Watley.
Callum.K	Oh, yeah.
Callum Morris	Oi, Ashley-Meakin Tatton, stop talking about me.
Ashley.T	I was't, that's your bag, isn't it?
Daniel Pegg	It's not Callum's, Ashley. It says at the front Gareth.
Oliver Sutton	That's Callum's. It says Callum Morris there it's been crossed out.
Callum.M	Yes, Daniel! I'm telling Mr. Eves.
Goerge Hunt	Don't! Callum. Go to Mr. Birks and tell him.
Alex Thorpe	He might get sacked.
Andrew Hall	Who will he believe, though? Mr. Eves or us?
Emily Dixon	Mr. Eves.
Emily.J	So, we need to pro-
Mr. Eves	STOP YOUR OWN CONVERSATION AND LISTEN TO WHAT I HAVE TO

SAY! Do you understand? Right, we are
doing science about volcanoes. Listen.

Everybody went quiet. But nobody was paying any
attention to Mr. Eves. They were all in their own world.
Thinking.

scene Three

It is morning break. Emily.J, Shinji, Luke and Joe.W are gathered round, talking.

Joe.W	What were you saying?
Emily.J	We need to prove to Mr. Birks that Mr. Eves has stolen Callum's bag.
Luke.H	And Emily Watley's purse. But we've got enough proof.
Emily.J	No, we haven't.
Shinji	Mr. Birks will never believe us. Let alone sack Mr. Eves.

Callum.M joins in.

Callum.M	We have got enough proof. He stole my bag.
Luke.H	Callum, go away.

Callum.M	Why should I?
Joe.W	Because you should.
Shinji	We are trying to sort somethings out here.
Emily.J	Yes! Well said. For you and Emily.W.
Callum.M	Oh, all right then. (still muttering Callum goes away)

Joe Sullivan comes over with Emily Watley.

Joe.W	Hello, how can I help you?
Emily.W	You should do something about this quick. I need to catch a bus and all my money's in my purse.
Joe.S	Why don't we just tell Mr. Birks?
Luke.H	We could just have a go.
Shinji	Yeah.

Rebecca comes running.

Rebecca	I don't care what you will say, but I'm telling Mr. Birks about this. This is so unfair.

Emily.W	What is it?
Rebecca	Gareth Pen knocked Emily Dixon over, right? Eves saw that, then. Guess what he did, called Gareth Pen, Emily Dixon and Chelsie over. You won't believe this. Eves actually gave Gareth Pen merits. He told Emily.D to write lines. He told Chelsie to write lines as well.
Emily.J	Why Chelsie?
Rebecca	I don't know.
Shinji	I'm reporting to Mr. Birks.
Emily.J	We'll take Callum.M, Emily.W, Becky.W with us. Do you want to come Joe.W and Luke?
Luke.H	No. Me and Joe will stay.
Shinji	All right then. I'll get Callum Morris.

scene Four

They are outside their classroom.

Rebecca	I'm going to check on Emily.

In the classroom

Shinji	Are you all right, you two?
Emily.D	I suppose so.
Chelsie Hill	I hope so. What have I done wrong? I haven't done anything, but I have to write lines.
Callum.M	We're talking to Mr. Birks, come on. Em and Chels.
Emily.D	No.
Chelsie.H	We might get into trouble.
Emily.D	Mr. Eves will smack us.
Emily.W	He won't.

Emily.J	Not in front of Mr. Birks.
Chelsie.H	I'm going then.
Emily.D	Me too.

Half way to Mr. Birks office

Shinji	Are you sure this is a good idea?
Emily.W	Just come on. I need my purse back by the end of the day.
Emily.J	It's not going to be that easy.

Outside Mr. Birks office

Rebecca	You knock, Cal.
Callum.M	No, Emily Jeff should do it because it was her idea after all.
Emily.J	No, it was't.
Shinji	I'll do it.

Shinji knocks.

Mr. Birks	Come in.

They all go in.

Mr. Birks	Yes?
Rebecca	Um... Shinji, you tell him.
Shinji	W-Well, it's a about Mr. Eves.
Emily.J	Yes, we've come to complain about him.
Mr. Birks	What about him?
Emily.W	Mr. Eves has got my purse and um... he's got Callum Morris's bag.
Chelsie.H	We think he stole it.
Rebecca	And he gave Gareth merits for knocking Emily.D over.
Emily.D	He made me write lines.
Chelsie.H	And me.
Emily.W	And Chelsie's done. NOTHING wrong. She was playing with Rose and Luce.
Mr. Birks	Are you making this up? If you are, I haven't got time for it.
Callum.M	We're not making it up.
Emily.W	We'll show you if you want.
Shinji	We will. It was on Mr. Eves' suitcase.
Mr. Birks	If you must. The rest of you are stay here except for Emily Wa and Shinji.

Emily.J   Okay.

Mr. Birks, Shinji and Emily.W go out of Mr. Birks office.

Rebecca   What if it's not there?

Emily.J   We're going to be in such a big trouble.

Mr Birks call after them.

Mr. Birks   You lot in my office, go out to break!

Rebecca   Okay.

Inside the classroom

Emily.W   It was there somewhere.

Shinji   It's here look, here–where is it? I'm sure
               it was here. Wasn't it?

Emily.W   Yeah, on Mr. Eves' suitcase. I just
               remember it.

Shinji   Mr. Eves' suitcase isn't here so -

Mr. Birks   Look, I really don't have the time. Stop
               messing about and have some break and
               give me some break as well!

Emily.W	Okay.

Mr. Birks goes out of the classroom.

Shinji	Why did you say "Okay"?
Emily.W	There was no choice.
Shinji	Yes there was! We could have said that we weren't messing about. Now, he'll think that we were messing.
Emily.W	Ok, then. We'll go and tell him.
Shinji	We'll go and see the others before we do that.

On the playground

Joe.W	There you are! We've solved part of the... what's the word?
Luke.H	Mystery.
Emily.J	Problem.
Joe.W	Whatever it is, we've solved part of it.
Rebecca	We think we have.
Shinji	Get on with it.
Luke.H	You know Gareth Pen?

Shinji	Yes very well. The thing we all know about him is bad influenced Year Six boy. He probably is a thief.
Emily.W	From hell. (giggles)
Shinji	Emily May Watley. I hope you haven't overheard what I was saying.
Emily.W	I have but I agree with ya.
Emily.J	Do you mind going away?

Emily Watley runs away.

Shinji	Get on with it.
Luke.H	Where was I?
Shinji	About Gareth Pen.
Luke.H	We think Mr. Eves is a very close relative to Gareth.
Joe.W	Very, very close.
Emily.J	Gaz dose look like Mr. Eves. Both of them look evil.
Luke.H	Emily's purse and Callum's bag, we don't think Mr. Eves stole them for himself. I think he stole them for Gaz.
Shinji	Prove it. I don't really get it.

Joe.W	First of all, if Gareth steals things off people, he'll get told off.
Emily.J	Yes, so if Eves does it for him, no one will ever tell him off.
Rebecca	Nobody will even think he did it.
Luke.H	that's reason one.
Shinji	Reason two?
Joe.W	If Eves and Pen are really relatives, they should like each other. And I'm sure that works on them as well.
Luke.H	So, when Gareth did the wrong thing, he gave Pen merits. Because they like each other-
Shinji	Because they are close relatives. Gotcha! Genius!

The bell rings.

Emily.J	Time to hear from you! How did it go?

Emily Watley comes running.

Emily.W	Can I join you please?

Shinji	Join me at dinner time in the field. We'll discuss things there. Tell you all about it then.
Emily.J	Okey Dokey.

scene Five

The class were working in silence. Each person's hands were aching with pain. People were losing their temper as they saw sheet after sheet to copy in their books. They got more annoyed and irritated minute by minute seeing Mr. Eves sipping coffee, his legs stretched out on the teacher's desk and over to Callum Kerr's.

Callum.K   Stinky feet.

A person can have so much patience. And they just can't help it when they have a person sitting in the room as relaxed as anything telling them off about things that didn't even exist to be told off. Things like: Put your glasses off! How dare you to have blonde curls, Hill? and Why do you have blue eyes, Dixon? Disgusting, put them off! and such like.

Rebecca	I've copied three sheets in my best handwriting. He's telling me to do it all over again, stupid old man?
Emily.D	Rather like stupid young man. I'm on my sixth sheet.
Rebecca	Shut up, Emily. How many sheets have we got?
Emily.D	Looks like over ten to me.
Lucie	It's over twenty because Callum Kerr's on his twenty first sheet.
Rebecca	I sometimes wonder if he can do magic.
Amy	Shinji's on twenty second sheet.
Rebecca	She must be a better witch.
Mr. Eves	Who's whispering? I've got a better ear than you think.
Rebecca	(In a tiny voice) Wasn't me. Don't look at me!

To everyone's delight, (except for Mr. Eves who enjoyed the lesson thoroughly) it is dinner time.

Joe.W	Awww. Ouch. My hand, It's hurting. O~u~c~h!

Luke.H   You'll Live! Even if you've not got your writing hand!

scene Six

After dinner Shinji, Luke, Joe.W, Rebecca, Emily.J and Emily.W met.

Joe.W	What happened? And good news?
Shinji	(moodily) No. It didn't go too well.
Rebecca	Oh dear. What happened?
Shinji	Well, Mr. Birks and me and Emily Watley went to our classroom. But Mr. Eves' suitcase and the purse was not in sight. So, he went off. Told us to go outside and stop messing around.
Emily.W	And she keeps nagging me because I said yes!
Luke.H	No wonder! He'll think we were messing around.
Shinji	That's exactly what I said. (sighs) We'll have to try again, somehow. I'm not

	giving up.
Luke.H	I'm definitely NOT.
Joe.W	Me too.
Emily.J	No way I'm going to give up!
Rebecca	I'm not giving up.
Emily.W	I'm not too sure anymore. I don't want to do this stuff anymore. Our reports are coming next Tuesday. What if Mr. Birks puts stuff like she's got big nose and suspects teachers for crime.
Shinji	You're just not confident in yourself. You know Mr. Eves is a thief. You've seen it yourself.
Luke.H	Your purse on Mr. Eves' desk? Isn't that enough proof that somebody is a thief?
Rebecca	You are boring. Go home. Emily Watley.
Emily.J	Yeah, go home. We don't want you, now. Not anymore.
Joe.W	Bye Bye. See you in classroom. Good BYE!
Emily.W	Huh! Fine. I know when I'm not wanted. You are all babish and foolish people. Playing games.

Shinji	WE are NOT playing GAMES!
Rebecca	Why do we bother to find her purse? I don't care anymore whether she goes home on a bus or walks or gets her purse back.
Joe.W	Neither do I. Can't be bothered.
Luke.H	Why don't we JUST find Callum Morris's bag?
Emily.J	Good Idea.
Emily.W	See if I care. I'll find it myself and I'll find it before you! Watch me. (She walks off)
Luke.H	Sorry but I don't want to watch your ugly face.
Rebecca	Or your fat belly.
Joe.W	Or your big, smelly, hairy bum!

They all laugh.

Emily.J	We need to come up with a plan that is sure to work.
Joe.W	You'll never know if it's going to work. Anything could happen.
Rebecca	Mmm.

Shinji	We should really have another step. Let's see if Mr. Eves is here with Callum's bag.
Luke.H	Yeah. Me and Shinji will go and have a look. Then if it's there, we will go to Mr. Birks and tell him.
Emily.J	Doesn't seem to work. But that's the only choice.
Shinji	Okay, see you!

Shinji and Luke come back later.

Luke.H	Mr. Eves hasn't got it. His suitcase is there but no sign of a bag.
Rebecca	LOOK! LOOK! Gareth has got the purse and the bag! There!
Joe.W	Oh yeah! Let's go and tell the dinner lady.
Emily.J	Mrs. Forst, Gareth has got Emily Watley's purse and Callum Morris's bag. We've been looking for it everywhere!
Mrs. Forst	Are you sure?
ALL	YES!

Mrs. F	GARETH?
Gareth	Yes, Mrs. Forst.
Mrs. F	These Year 5s are saying that, that purse and that bag you've got is theirs.
Gareth	I don't get you.
Rebecca	Yes, you do!
Mrs. F	I don't know. I'll hand these two properties to Mr. Eves. He can sort it out. Fair enough.
Rebecca	But-
Luke.H	Sshh! Yes, it's fair enough. Mrs. Forst.
Emily.J	LUKE! It isn't fair enough. You just... let go of the glorious chance.
Joe.W	Why on earth did you do that, Luke?
Shinji	Mmmm. Maybe Luke was right to do that. If we kept arguing with her, she might get cross with us and just give the properties.
Rebecca	I still think you two are CRAZY.
Joe.W	And MAD.
Emily.J	Oh well. When something's done, you can't change it.
Rebecca	What do we do now?
Shinji	Just wait and see Mr. Eves sort things out.

Emily.J	Rather strange things in.
Joe.W	OH NO! Mr. Eves never sorts ANYTHING out, does he? Hope Mrs. Forst gave the job to Mr. Birks.
Luke.H	Only that didn't happen.
Joe.W	OH NO! OH NO~~~!

scene Seven

Rebecca	There's no need for us to sit here is there? Let's go to the classroom. And see what Eves do!
Joe.W	Let's go.

They all go to the their classroom.

Emily.J	Look! There are the purse and the bag!
Shinji	A glorious chance! Get a thick black pen.
Rebecca	What are you going to do?
Shinji	Write on the purse, Emily.W, real big.
Luke.H	The same with Callum's?
Shinji	Go on. Then we'll take these to Mr. Birks.
Joe.W	Nice one!
Emily.J	Do it quick before Eves comes.

Shinji and Luke write it and go to Mr. Birks.

Shinji	Mr. Birks! Look, this is Emily.W and Callum.M's bag that was on Mr. Eves's desk.
Emily.J	We are not lying. You must believe us.
Joe.W	Whole of our class will prove it. Please believe us.
Rebecca	You have -
Mr. Birks	Ok. I believe that purse is Emily's and that bag is Callum's. Now, go away.
Luke.H	No, Mr. Birks. We don't want you to believe that. We want you to believe that Mr. Eves is a thief.
Mr. Birks	If he is a thief?
Shinji	You will have to mmm.
Joe.W	Sack him. Definitely! You don't want a thief to teach us, do you?
Luke.H	You believe us, don't you?
Mr. Birks	Please, you just don't suspect teachers like that.
Joe.W	Mr. Birks, we are talking the truth really. If we made it up... we would never be in here being serious with you.

Mr. Birks	Follow me. All of you.

They go into their clsaaroom. They all sit round a table.

Mr. Birks	Tell me the whole story, please-
Luke.H	Right.
Mr. Birks	Rebecca, tell me the story.
Rebecca	Right, it was just a normal morning. we went into the classroom. Mr. Eves came in saying that Miss Cross is ill. Mr. Eves sat down on the chair and put his suitcase on the desk. Luke and Joe noticed the purse and bag. And the purse was Emily's and the bag was Callum Morris's. So... and we didn't like Mr. Eves. We wanted him sacked. So we wanted to tell you that Mr. Eves is a thief and that's that.
Mr. Birks	What about the story that you told me that Gareth Eves knocked Emily Dixon over?
Rebecca	Did you Say Gareth EVES?
Luke.H	He wasn't Gareth Pen?
Mr. Birks	That's not his real name though.

Joe.W	We've sorted all of it out!! Now we are sure Gareth is a relative of Mr. Eves.
Shinji	Goody!
Emily.J	What we've sorted out is that Mr. Eves doesn't steal things for himself but for Gareth.
Joe.W	Because Gareth is poor.
Mr. Birks	Well, that makes sense. But I just can't sack a teacher, believing you, guys.
Luke.H	Oh, (nods) So it ends worth nothing right?
Rebecca	Sad. We've tried ever so hard.

There's a silence. But Amy Plant runs in, Screaming.

Amy	Mr. Birks! Look out of the window! Mr. Eves!
Emily.J	What's happening?
Shinji	Oh no. Jack's only Year 2. Mr. Eves is hitting him so hard. Mr. Birks, do something. Poor Jack.

scene Eight

In Mr. Birks office

Police 1	So what happened?
Mr. Birks	Well, this man, Mr. Eves as a teacher he has stolen children's properties and hitting little children.
Police 2	We'll sort him out in police station. Not to give any trouble, Bye!
Mr. Birks	Thanks Very much.
Shinji, Emily.J, Luke, Joe.W, Rebecca	Thank you!
Mr. Birks	Well, thanks to you lot too.
All	Your welcome!
Emily.W	Oh, you lot! I've just come to tell you, you're in the newspaper. And you'll get £10 each. Congratulations.
Luke.H	Thanks for the news.

Rebecca	Emily Watley I think you have something to say, don't you?
Joe.W	Yeah, we found your purse!
Emily.W	Oh, Thank you!

university, life, job -Lucy's life

Lucy was thirteen. Tomorrow she would be fourteen. So after the summer holiday she would be in the middle school. Edward's middle school. It was the biggest school in the town. She felt a bit nervous. There was another reason she felt nervous because her best friend Abigail was going to move down to London. And then she was left on her own. No friend to walk to school with.

It was an evening. A normal one. But Lucy felt this evening was special. She felt sleepy and went to her bedroom and lied down on her bed. The moon shone down. She thought. Tomorrow's my birthday and the day after that I would be in Edward's middle school. All alone. She tried to forget and went to sleep.

She was standing still when somebody called her. "Lucy~!" She looked around, there was an adult calling her. She realised she was an adult too!

And the big building behind her was... Cambridge University!

So she was in Cambridge University and Abigail calling her!

"Abigail! It's been a long time I have seen you!"

"Oh, Lucy wake up! We were at the barber's together a minute ago!"

"Were we? Never mind where we were then." Lucy spoke casually.

"Let's go..." Lucy interrupted Abbi.

"Where?"

"What's wrong with you today? We've got our audition to be a popstar!"

Lucy was shocked. An audition to be a popstar? She didn't even know what song they were singing. But then she remembered. She was in the future now. So she must have practiced much!

At the audition Lucy was nervous, when it was their turn. But like magic she sang so well. Lucy wondered if she was actually singing. That day, Lucy and Abbi were picked and they became a popstar called Orange!

Lucy woke up with a happy smile. Even though her best friend was away, when she was at the university and be a popstar! Her dream would be coming true!!!

you have a diary?
I have chicky!!!

It was a fine afternoon. Sarah was going to the library to read some books. On the way she was tripped over by something.

"Ow- what is it?"

It was a pink diary. It was locked but Sarah was able to open it with her fingernails. She met her friend Bomi in the library.

"Hey Bomi! Look at this... It's somebody's diary!" Sarah yelled in excitement.

"Wow!! Who's is it? It belongs to Rosie Bell... It's Rosie's. Let's give it back to her. It looks like a secret diary. She will be really upset."

"C'mon, Bomi. Let's read some of it. Have some fun!"

"But it's a secret diary. We can't read someone's secrets. That's mean. We know who's it is. Well~ I'm not reading." And she went away. Sarah began reading it.

July 14th Weather: Nice

It was really sunny day. I was in the field with Annabel just talking. Then I heard somebody says 'Rose the fatty'. I looked around.

Sarah and others were laughing. I bet a million pounds it was Sarah. Annabel said don't be so upset because it would be only a joke but I can't help feeling so upset today!! I don't blame Sarah... I blame myself being so fat to be a fun... My feeling doesn't match with the weather today.

July 15th Weather: Horrible

Today's weather was really horrible but I felt good today. It seems like whenever I don't feel good, the weather is nice. But when the weather is horrible, I feel really good. The reason I feel good today is I am in acting class after school. A lot of my friends do it. Well, not my friends but boys from our class. Joe, Louisen, Tom, Oliver...

It's all boys most of them but we have girls too. Nelly, Chelsie, Melanie... They are all the girls I know. They were practising a play. It was Cinderella!! Oliver was the prince!! Mr. Suwon said I will be in the next play called Thumb princess. A play that has been changed a little from the real one. He said he would make me Thumbelina's mother. I am so happy. But I am sorry for Annabel who isn't in acting classes. If she took the acting class with me it would have been really fantastic. A pity that is real pity.

Sarah was impressed by Rosie's diary. And she really felt sorry for Rosie when she teased her she was fat. Sarah decided to make a diary and write in it when she gave Rosie her diary back.

And she wrote a diary herself. It was a yellow one. It didn't have a lot of paper in it. So Sarah supposed she won't be able to write long in this diary but started scribbling.

August 2nd ☼
The weather in boiling hot today. I've had three ice creams already but I am still hot. Wouldn't there be a way? To cool my body??
Yeah! A great way to cool··· in having a sleepover party···
With your friends that is brilliant. So I decided to have a

sleepover party at Bomi's. Bomi's parents let Bomi have as many friends around her house.

So we could take as many people we want to!!

So, me, Bomi, Lilly, Michael, Tom, Melanie, Harry and Jumbo created a sleepover party. I felt so fabulous. It was so exciting!!

So the eight of us walked to Bomi's house. Bomi's parents greeted us. We watched a horror movie. There were so disgusting parts and really scary parts too. We all sat together in a sofa that only three people can sit. I was in the middle between Lily and Bomi. It was really squashing. We slept in Bomi's room. Bomi had a really small room. And her brother had a big room. So we slept in her brother's room!! Bomi got told off but she said it didn't really matter··· She's a tough one if you ask me!! It is the middle of night now. It's about 4 am now. But I can't sleep. I don't want to sleep. I think everybody's like that. They are all sitting up eating snacks except Lilly and Harry snoring in the coner. And I am scribbling in the corner. Bomi is scribbling away on her brother's desk. Bet she's got a diary too. Melanie and Jumbo are talking so loudly. Lilly woke up. The last one to wake up. Michael is sleeping again. Tom too. Jumbo and Lilly are asleep again. I think Bomi and Melanie are getting to bed too. So I suppose I will sleep too. Hang on! Before I go to sleep, I want to make you a name. I am gonna call you Chicky. Because you are yellow hey?

Then good night Chicky!!

EVERY DAY

EVERY DAY

Personal Details

Name	ShinJi Park
Age	10(Year 5)

Favourite

Colour	Blue
Food	Pizza, Cake, Rice and Chicken
Author	Roald Dahl, Enid Blyton, Jacqueline Wilson
Pop band	Hear'Say, S Club 7

List of friends and teachers, I know!

CHRIST CHURCH JUNIOR(My Old School)
Abigail, Se-young, Sera, Amy Shart, Beccy, Aarani,
Shin-ae, Sian, Nadia, Jamie, Laura, Mary, Hannah,
Groria, Amy Salt, Sabinah, Rebecca, Lucy

ST MARY'S (My New School)
Amy Plant, Emily Jeffrey, Rebecca, Rosie, Emily
Whatley, Lucy B, Poppy, Lucia, Chelsie

Teachers at Christ Church Junior
Miss Field, Mrs Macnaughton, Miss Howard, Mr Moss,
Mr Attfield(Head), Mrs Shah, Mrs Page,

Teachers at St Mary's
Mr Rushton, Mr Wilson, Miss Cross, Mrs Queen,
Mrs Edward, Mrs Wakeham

Wood Croft First School   Kids / Teacher
Mr Tappley(Head), Mrs Daughtry, Mrs Karini
Carla, Sara P, Amelia, Goerginah, Hannah, Hailey,
Eilghly

1

Hi! I'm ShinJi. Hard name eh? But don't laugh. Anyway there is no reason why you should be laughing about my name, there's no reason why you should.

Well I'm a goody-goody in the school, quite bored of goody-goodies. Hey?

Tomorrow is Friday and I'm really looking forward to go to school on Monday. This is half term and how I miss the school badly. I have lots of friends well, not lots just few girls. Amy, Emily, Rebecca, and few more girls. I'm not bullied or else, no one dose in the school. It's not a posh school. The school hasn't got enough texts.

No one dare can read this. I will scream and yell if they do apart from my permission. Well I will not give anybody a permission.

Why should I? When it's a private book?

Hey mate, I got to get ready for my bed. I don't want my mum bothering saying get ready, Do I?

Your name is um... Super-Duper name like mine, How about:

① Sweetie   ② Sabrina

③ Matey   ④ Friend

Sweetie's too funny, Sabrina's too girly. Hey, How about Matey that seems cool than Friend. Friend is a cool name too. I have a diary called Friend.

Tell you lots and lots tomorrow.

Mum's calling me to get ready for my bed and I will. I'm too tired.

NIGHTIE NIGHTIE

2

Hello?

Hey Matey, I feel really dizzy, everything seems to me is spinning round and round for ever.

My dad and mum, me and my brother went to council today. How boring it was. My dad and mum had a long long conversation. All the thing seemed to be reminding again and again. Boring Council!

We spent hours and hours there no more then hours much much more yes, A hundred years well, at least it seemed.

I'm getting really bored and is scribbling down.

The time gose s~o s~l~o~w~l~y. I hope I had somebody to play my precious Scrabble with me. But my brother is busy with homework. And mum is preparing for our meals. No one seems to be bored except me. I don't want to do that or this or anything.

Boring world. No, this is wrong. The world can be ever so exciting like whole world is made of chocolate.

3

Hey, I thought of something not at all boring. Writing funny stories. I got a notebook of my favourite story(well it used to be). And I could carry on writing it. Well, I will do that I will scribble down later see ya!

I'm back. I couldn't scribble on the other notebook, because I couldn't find it. I saw it yesterday but I can't see it now. I searched near the window sill. It wasn't there that's where I saw it. So I went under the bed. I took the box out and searched in there.

There was my glass teddy bear wrapped carefully with tissue paper and a Disney Land magazine and a lot of cards and some sort- of- board games. But no notebook. So, I just started scribbling here on you with my pencil. I decided what I'll do. I will play a game of my own with a board game in the box, teacher game. That is one of my hobbies. I do it almost everyday.

See ya in a bit! I'll scribble when I got bored! See U! (real one)

4

Hey, what I wrote yesterday about my friend is quite wrong. Because I don't think I'm Rebecca's friend. Because I do not like her one bit. When I tried to play teacher game with sort- of- board game before I settled I got bored. After that, I got ever so bored. So, I just went down to dining room and my mum was watching (well, reading really) her book.

I didn't know what to do. So I just wondered round the dining room. "Are you hungry?" asked mum. I was a bit hungry then so I said "yes". My mum asked me if I wanted some toast, I said I would like to have some cornflakes. So I did. And I came up. Here I am. I am scribbling. What on earth am I going to do now???!!!

I started drawing in my special drawing pad. That was sensible idea. I drew 4 girls. Cool girls. With lots of make ups, Elisa, Laura, Jamie and Claire. Then I went off to my brother's room to get scissors. But they weren't there. He was doing math work book and I asked him where the scissors were. Then I disturbed him a teeny weeny bit. And he kicked me and so did I. Mum said "What's the matter?" So I stopped the fighting and went down to the dining room.

I sat on a sofa doing nothing after a while. When I calmed myself a bit, I went off to my room to do my math work book to catch him up. But I couldn't concentrate. So I just started drawing silly pictures round it.

Mum called us for dinner and our family had dinner. Then I stayed in the living room (double dining room) to watch the telly. When I got a bit bored of watching the telly, of course I went to my room. And I started reading for ages. Now here I am scribbling down what I've done. I'm too tired without any reason. After all~

Alas, I forgot something before I went on reading for ages. I played my precious scrabble with my brother. And Guess What! I've Won!!!

I have beat him. My brother Jae(his real name is Jae Hyung) looked a bit embarrassed~ Ha Ha! Jae scored 118 and I scored 119!

I'll carry on the sentence there I was trying to write.

I'm too tired without any reason. After all today has been a wonderful day. Bye! Good night! MATEY!!

5

Hi, Matey. I just think time has gone so fast. I have been reading 'Charlie and The Chocolate Factory' for ages. Then I started drawing. It is super. A visitor came round our house. He was very tall. I cannot remember him clearly now. Because it was first time I've met him! He lives in Keele and I live in Leek, it is tiny bit far away. When he had gone, I had to do some work book. Because I have played all the morning. Then I watched the telly for ages until now. A lot of programmes real fun ones quizes and stuff. Mum said we're going out early to the city, Hanley early morning. So we had to go sleep quite early.

And my legs are aching. Hey Mate! Do you know something? I got 5 dolls in my bed sleeping with me! Ones a big one A dog called Fushu. Next one is another dog called Dalmaciane and another dog called Pelly(Jonny his old name) fourth one is a mini called Starsaura(Clowy Mini her old name). And last one is a gorilla from Tarzan. He(Well, actually She) is called Slicy. I like them all. Slicy got light I can switch on. That's why I like Him(Her).

My legs, Ouch, is aching aching . Good night, Bye, Mate!

6

Hiya! Today has been a cool day, Mate. In the morning we went to Hanley. First we went to Pottery Shopping Centre. There, first we went into Waterstone. Mum bought us English answer book each. Then we went to another shop, but I can't remember it's name. Then we went to Disney store. Cool. Next, We went to Stationery box and mum bought me cool yellow carry bag and an index book red one.

Then we walked all the way to the Festival park, we ate our lunch from Mcdonald's. There was full of people. I and Jae waited ages for a spare table. At last we had a table to sit. From Mcdonald's I got a plastic doll from Disney ATLANTIS THE LOST EMPIRE. She is pretty. I hadn't thought of choosing her a name. I'm sure there will be a name is the tilno. But It will take too long to find her proper name. So, I'll decide one. How about!

① Amy   ② Rebecca   ③ Emily

I don't think I'll do Amy. Because I already got a Mini called Amy. Rebecca's pretty and so is Emily too. But I think Rebecca suits her more than Emily. So, Her name is REBECCA.

After that we went into Toys R Us. I tried on the Halloween mask and my mum said I looked quite scary. We watched all round the store. I tried the activity computer and lots of other things. It was a fun.

Next, Mum and I was desperate for toilet. So, we went into mum care world and went to toilet. After that we went into footwear. But all the shoes were too expensive so we walked back to Hanley. We done some shopping in Tesco then went home. After I've finished writing, I'll play with Rebecca and then go to bed.

Good night! Alas! There will be 6 dolls sleeping with me!

7

Hi Mate! In the morning we met sister Yun(She's not my sister or something just neighbour but I call her sister Yun). We went to Chineese market then we went to Newcastle Pizza Hut. The pizza was Yummy Yummy. I got three crayons from Pizza Hut. Then we went to Sainsbury and went home. Next we went to Wilkinson. My mum bought toilet thing and dad bought toothpast and shampoo.

And Guess What! I bought some underwear! I needed 9-10 but there wasn't one. So I bought 7-8. It will be ever so short! Well I'll like that. Jae bought nothing but he didn't complain. Because he was in quite a good mood. When we finished shopping in Wilko, we went to Safeway. Safeway was decorated with Pumpkins, Spider, Skeletons because the Halloween is coming! We bought some sweets incase somebody came to our house for sweets. Because last Halloween we hadn't bought any sweets. Because we had some, but soon we were running out of sweets! Bye-Bye! Mum's calling me for dinner.

8

Hello! I'm back for writing this holiday. Remember? This was an holiday diary. Last night it snowed and snowed and I was glad it did. Because I had a lovely winter time making a toddler snowman and playing snow fight with my brother, Jae. Remember when he was a pest? But if I get on with him very well it is a superb fun to play with somebody then playing on your own.

I've just finished reading a book. And I've decided something I will try to be good and study in my spare time. The other thing I've decided is to eat decent food. All these things are for my great future. I don't want to be called bad bold girl like Elizabeth who was in the story. And I don't want to be bad and unclever. Elizabeth was very clever and turned out to be good. My last promised. I'll never want to be called Shorty when I grow up full stop.

The final promise I'm trying to make is I won't quarrel with anyone. Because if you do, your face will turn ugly. If you quarrel, that means you're disliking somebody. So you won't smile and won't make yourself prettier. You must not judge people with their faces and looks. It doesn't matter whether their heart is bad. They must turn their heart into a good heart first than their looks.

It must have been boring. But I think I should try not to quarrel and make myself as good as gold.

Good bye! Night Night.

9

I'm back! It's a long time passed since I wrote. Dunno, why don't you question me? I'm a bit lazy.

Urgh! Just when I started. Need the loo! See you later!

I'm back! Ergh! I left this book open! Jae might have seen it! It's suppose to be private. And I'm a bit embarrassing because about this goody goody stuff. Shouldn't have thought about that. I never seem to keep promises I didn't even remember about it. Talk about embarrassing. It's just over Easter and I didn't even manage to have a single egg. Talk about embarrassing again! I had to say I didn't know how many eggs I had. I've been going round to Poppy's house. The second time I met Pop's dad was really different, you know. First time I went he was all kind and friendly and everything but not the second time. Wouldn't even let Pops giggle when we were watching Simpsons! When I was round at her place I found 2 abandoned eggs and Pops found 1. Pops took out a nest from somewhere to put the eggs in. We place the nest a the branches well Pops did. She was trying to get over it and I bet she shook the nest a bit. (We had 2 eggs then.) One cracked and the other one was safe in the leaves. She started blaming me then. Talk about Unfair!

Matey, from lots of experiences.

I managed to learn and hear the life is unfair.

It was Jae's birthday tomorrow. Urghhh!

I'm getting mad. I meant yesterday by the way. I keep talking about Poppy aren't I?

Well Pops and Lu(Lucia) are my best friends now. I've told nobody, no one at all why this happened. Only Amy and Emily and myself know. But I bet I could trust you to keep it a secret. Well, it was like this. Well at school there was this Pop Idol thingy. Amy and Emily were going for playing Clarinet. So they rehearsed but I got out of their way and hung around with Rosie S and Lucie B or Poppy H and Lucia C. They thought I was ignoring them. One wet break. Aim(Amy) called me over to talk. She said "We think you are ignoring us." rocking her chair as if she knew half of me. I said "What do you mean?" and I put on a puzzled voice and face. I knew what she meant all right. I had a lump in my throat and all. So that's why I said that. Then she said "Oh noth-ing!" With you–know–nothing–and–I–know–every-thing expression and voice.

And one day eventually they said it. Beginning with you know what happened to Becky thing and I was glad that morning came they're boring people they are. Play-ing tick every day. Every break unless they are playing colour TICK! That's that.

It was Jae's birthday yesterday. I remember saying that I'll carry on with that subject. Mum bought double choc gataeu(How do you spell it???) and from 'Toys R Us' his present. Not fair. He got two stuffs and I only got one stuff. Only 8 pounds. It was watch and I was satis-fied then, but not now. Jae has this Digimon thingy and a Umbro pencil case. Huh! Mum bought us an ice cream each as a special treat. I didn't have a special treat as an ice cream or something. I wasn't bothered because the ice cream was yummy, yummy! Jae's birthday cake is making my mouth water. The most incredible taste.

I watched some videos. We were supposed to be going out to somewhere. Fun day OUT not IN but Mum said it was too windy. So we watched Toy Story and three-quaters of Aladdin and 40 thieves. Sats is another thing. I want to write about. I've got some bad test nerves I have. It makes me feel awful because it's in 2 days and I haven't even revised. The only thing I wanted to say about it is wish me lucks! Cross your fingers per leeese!

I want to stop talking about it now. my eyes are blurry. I want to get on with my own Barbie meg. Night Night !

****

To Matey   From ShinJi, P.

ARE YOU
ShinJi Type or Jae Type?

When you are angry, how do you behave?
A: Oh leave them! It's their style.
B: Straight away, "Hey, you couldn't you Stop it?"

If you chose A, you are not very brave to say anything in front of somebody.

If you chose B, you have a mind that has to be your
way. But if it goes too far, it won't be good.

So if you choose A : Right, you are Jae style.
Hey B : mates! Congratulations! You are my type.

appendix

In addition, an appendix contains what she wrote
when she was university student.
She wrote these articles when she was a reporter
of 'Korea University English Magazine'. (2010~2013)

Surveillance:
My Friend and Enemy

The Korea University English Magazine

THE GRANITE TOWER(SEPTEMBER 2010)

By Park Shinji

She lives on a rather obscure alley near school. She usually tries to head home early, for she is scared that the cruelties she watches on the news everyday might become her own story. However, these days, she goes home late with an easy mind now that the Closed-Circuit Television(CCTV)s are installed in the alley. She deems CCTV as a key to prevent crimes to a certain extent. CCTVs are everywhere and she feels relaxed being with them. But when she coincidentally spots a nearly invisible CCTV from the hallway she always walked through, she shudders by the thought that she might be recorded without being aware of it. She begins to have second thoughts about where this society might be heading; the possibilities that it might transform itself into a spooky 'surveillance society'.

On July 11, Choi Cheol-ho, an actor, took the heat for assaulting a woman. He resigned the cast of Dong-Yi on his own wills and said that he will have time for self-restraint and self-reflection. Initially Choi denied all the charges but when the CCTV images of him kicking the woman was released on the news, he had no choices but admit his wrongdoing. On July 16, after 20 days the elementary school student rape case in Dongdaemun-gu happened, the criminal was arrested. The police stated that CCTV played a big role in specifying the suspect's personal information.

As seen from the two cases that grabbed social attention recently, the common denominator here is the CCTV. In both cases, CCTV held the key to uncovering the truth. As if to emphasize the necessity of CCTVs, two terrible crimes of Kim Kil-tae and Kim Soo-chul, cases, in which they abducted and raped elementary school students, occurred from places without surveillance cameras.

Brutal crimes are reported relentlessly day after day and people live in fear of being the next victim. Especially sexual violence against elementary school students has increased by 70% over the last four years. Naturally, the demand for CCTVs have drastically increased across the nation. The CCTV market is rapidly growing in response. Many Koreans have begun to consider the surveillance TV as one of must-have home appliances. "Usually, the CCTVs are high in demand from companies or stores but orders from ordinary homes have increased by 20% lately," says a salesperson.

As to supplement the policies regarding violent crimes, the government announced that it will establish integrated CCTV control centers. When the control centers begin operating, CCTVs that run separately will be under the control of one single center. Thus prompt collection of evidence and effective management of the machines will become available. Integrated control centers are planned to be installed in 249 cities by 2014.

The history of CCTV began in Germany in 1942 to observe rockets launching. The surveillance cameras were first used publicly to reduce crime rates in Oleans, New York, 26 years later. Ever since then, they have been widely used in shops and companies alike. Not only have they been widely used, but they are also evolving into higher levels of technology. For one, a CCTV connected to emergency pager is planned to be introduced to children specifically. If a child senses an emergency he can send signals by his pager equipped with GPS. Then the CCTV will rotate itself to the place the signal was emitted. Moreover, through smartphones and personal computers, people can also watch CCTV screens. Surveillance cameras with artificial intelligence are another good example of an 'evolving' CCTV.

The main public usage of CCTV is linked to crime-preventing it and managing it after the crime occurred. According to a survey, 50% of the prisoners answered that they hesitate to commit a crime when there are surveillance TVs a nearby. The recording to CCTVs are frequently used in searching out the criminal. Most of the postings related to CCTV on Koreapas, a Korea University Internet Community, were about utilizing CCTV screens to identify criminals. Some users posted their experiences of searching the criminal with CCTV or asked other users how to use the CCTV to identify the criminal for their lost property.

"I approve of surveillance cameras, for I believe that public interests come first in public places. A bit of privacy intrusion at the cost of safety is bearable. Also, I think that CCTVs play a big role in tracking down a criminal," says Park Song-won('10, International language and literature). "As long as they do not intrude my private spaces, CCTVs are necessary for safety issues," she added.

This CCTV wasn't working. The terrorist still is.

When asked about the installation of CCTVs inside school campus, Kim Min-Kyu('10, Foreign language and literature) replied. "It doesn't matter much as long as the

CCTVs are not installed in changing rooms and bathroom." Reflecting on cases where individual properties are stolen in campus, he thinks that CCTVs come in handy when fighting such crimes. "The original purpose of installing CCTV is to prevent crimes so I do not oppose to the purpose of installing them," he continued. Concerning human right issues about CCTVs, he added that for ordinary people like him there are no human rights being abused.

Contrarily, some express discomfort to the idea that they are being watched. "I acknowledge the benefits CCTV can have on the whole so I am partially for their usage. Nevertheless, I feel inconvenient with CCTVs that are randomly installed, such as those set up in Daramjigil," said Kim Jae-Hyung('07, English Language and Literature). "CCTVs are installed inordinately so I sometimes feel that I do not have much personal life."

The assertions of the CCTV opposers should not be overlooked, for these are cameras permeated in our lives more than people seem to recognize. It is no exaggeration to say that we are being watched every second. The moment we step out of our house and get on the elevator, we start being watched. As we attempt to get on a subway or go to the parking lot for our cars, we are snapped once again. CCTVs record us when we enter convenience stores, stationery stores or any kind of shops. We are also being watched inside school as well. There are surveillance TVs inside and outside of reading rooms, on library halls and nearby lockers.

The permeation of CCTVs in our ordinary lives is ongoing. Though the recent trend tends to be in favor of CCTV, as a society, the problem is more complicated than the mere positive effect of preventing and solving crimes. Invasion of privacy is a main issue related to the problem. Also, there always exists the problem of misusing CCTV. It could turn into a serious problem if individual's privacy is utilized for commercial or personal benefits. Another problem is high dependence on CCTVs, making people become oblivious to the limitations of CCTVs. The simple but often forgotten limit of CCTV is that they are mostly scrutinized after everything has happened. Although there are CCTVs running, nobody actually watches them carefully, which is obviously an economic loss. Additionally, overdependence on machines can lead to reduction of work forces. Such dehiring can create a situation where there is not enough manpower to solve the problem even though a problem was spotted on CCTV.

A society with similar concerns is Britain. There are approximately 4.2 million CCTVs in Britain which means that it has one for every 14 citizens. Like any other countries, Britain resorted to CCTVs for usages related to crime. However, now it is notable that the machines have become deeply involved with the everyday lives of British citizens and that they are having a considerable influence on ordinary people's lives. Collection of private information has become easier, now that the technology has developed and made itself nearly invisible. In Britain, the CCTVs are more than intelligent. If lampposts(CCTV is installed inside the lamppost) spot people doing something socially inadequate, they shout at them. Many people are warning that Britain has "sleepwalked" to a surveillance society and has "woken up" to such a society. A society that records every move and every action its people take reminds many of the 'Big Brother Society' from George Orwell's 1984.

A lesson to be learned from the case of Britain: If we don't give second thoughts before rushing to install CCTVs all around us, we might go for wool and come home shorn. The advantages CCTVs can have in our life is undeniable, but too much can do us harm. It seems that 'being appropriate' might always be the best answer.

Festivity for Everyone

The Korea University English Magazine

THE GRANITE TOWER(OCTOBER 2010)

By Park Shinji

Hwajeong Tiger Dome(also known as the Hwajeong Gymnasium) is a grand gymnasium you spot as you head upwards behind the campus. For most people, you go there for your entrance ceremony and freshman orientation and that is about it. Nevertheless, various events that attract people from all over the country take place in Hwajeong. This is a positive thing for sure, but what if there were more activities held for Korea University(KU) students to enjoy together?

Strolling on campus, people approach you and ask you the way to Hwajeong Tiger Dome. Usually they do not look like KU students, but younger, around the age of middle or high school. And when you are on Chamsari-gil heading to Gaeunsa-gil, you can easily spot people(mostly female) holding up placards for their idols. Quite a number of fan meetings have been held in Hwajeong Tiger Dome. On August 7, SHiNee(a Korean quintet boy band) held their first fan meeting in Hwajeong. Following that, Park Jay Bum met his fans, also for the first time. Another grand fan meeting is scheduled for September 26 casting Girls' Generation, and as for this fan meeting, you might easily spot middle-aged male fans as well. Hwajeong Tiger Dome was also seen by TV audiences when the second preliminary round of

Superstar K, a famous Korean version of a singing competition program, "the American Idol," was held there.

The events mentioned are just to list a few. There are a variety of other events in addition to the celebrity fan meetings. School related events such as freshman orientations, entrance ceremonies and alumni meetings are also set up in Hwajeong Tiger Dome. Sports matches, concerts and job fairs are also events held there.

Hwajeong Tiger Dome, completed in 2006, was built as a multipurpose building, and has been successful in serving this role. According to its established aim, the diverse cultural and sporting events are meant to contribute to the growth of a creative campus culture. The schedule for Hwajeong Tiger Dome is quite hectic throughout the year. Some might wonder why Hwajeong Tiger Dome has to be booming all the time when it could be left in peace to promote the health of the students and faculty. The simplest reason to refute such an argument is to say that it is better to use it in some way than to simply waste it on nothing. Also, the economic benefits derived through renting it out go directly to the KU Financial Department and are then used for a variety of purposes. Moreover, because of the nature of universities, which are unlike other private-education institutions, KU has the duty to share what it can with the community at large. In that sense, hosting diverse cultural events for many to enjoy is one way to fulfill this duty.

"I believe that holding diverse outside events is okay," says Park Seo-Hee('10, Foreign Language and Literature). "However, there are not many events that KU students can actually participate in. If it is a 'university' gymnasium, it should have its own prescribed roles," continues Park. She suggests that it would be nice if there were art festivals or concerts hosted by school clubs.

All is good: it is best to make full use of the facilities; there are considerable economic benefits; and the university has the duty to share what it can with the public-these are all strong arguments in favor of the status quo. However, a fact that should not be overlooked is that students should come first, no matter what. They should always be considered when such big events are planned to be held in school facilities. There should be more cultural and sporting activities in which KU students can play the leading roles. At the least, the students should be given the opportunity to participate in some way.

Of course it would be necessary to admit the financial and organizational difficulties the school might incur if they were to meet such demands from KU students; nevertheless, it would be worth a try. If, under certain circumstances, we were given the opportunity to take part in diverse cultural and sporting activities, then it would not only be "their" festivity at Hwajeong, but "our" festivity, too-open to all, for all to enjoy.

Plan B; Peaceful and Democratic Solutions for Protests

The Korea University English Magazine

THE GRANITE TOWER(NOVEMBER 2010)

By Park Shinji

Gearing for the upcoming G20 Summit scheduled for November 11 and 12, Seoul is bustling with all the preparations and final checks. As the host of an international summit, the city is filled with hopes and excitements. However, as the history of globalization shows, this kind of affairs are always accompanied with protests. In a candlelight vigil against US beef imports last year, the police blasted demonstrators with water cannons. This time, having a big event ahead, they are back with sound cannons. Referring to their usage at Toronto, the police authorities claim that sound cannons are safe and cost-efficient. However, some safety issues concerning hearing impairment are still left unverified. The use of sound cannons is a hasty plan, and it should not be the solution for quelling demonstrations.

Sound cannons, or long range acoustic devices(LRAD), are usually capable of generating noise as loud as 150dB within 100 yards. They were used by American warships to warn vessels approaching the US territory without permission. The device, which was originally developed to be used at sea, is now found useful at land. Countries, such as the US and Canada, are purchasing the LRAD to fight against organized protesters.

Although the police officials say that LRADs are "non-lethal", they are still weapons. Therefore, it is natural for the public to question their safety. According to the police department, a research institute at Seoul National University(SNU) has validated LRAD's safety, but the result of trial performances turns out to be more alarming than their arguments. In trials, the LRAD shot 140dB noise for five seconds at 32m of distance. The journalists on the spot described the noise as unpleasant and piercing. Many complained that the sound is unbearable, and suffered from headaches and queasiness. Since the reporters did not shed any blood, would it be just to call it harmless? As the journalists' experience shows, the devices are capable of creating discomfort-sonic cannons are clearly hazardous.

Furthermore, a research institute at SNU has examined sonic cannons on the basis of technological efficiency, but not on the basis of harmfulness to humans. A professor at the research institute admitted that the reverberating noise can severely damage auditory organs and violently shake bowels. Even worse, a simulation of LRADs shows that the level of decibels amplifies in cities, because the sound is blocked by tall buildings.

Due to safety concerns, the use of LRADs in Toronto was limited and had clear statements of when it was allowed. When controversies regarding sound cannons piled up, Ontario Superior Court of Canada permitted the voice function of the cannon but restricted the alert function only to certain circumstances. Unfortunately, Korea has not yet established regulations against the LRADs. The lack of legal restraints raises serious concerns, because the unrestricted use of unconfirmed devices can put citizens in danger. Utilizing sound as weapons is ultimately an act of aggression-only bloodless. Violence calls for more violence, exacerbating the situation. In other words, a demonstration that started out peaceful could turn violent if what the police have in stock is armed intervention.

National mobilization of sound cannons as anti-protest devices is undemocratic, and the purpose of the mobilization is very much doubted. A demonstration, by definition, is a public act of expressing opposition to something. G20 protests could be considered as a mere assertion of opinions as they at the moment have not yet turned violent. Everyone can and should have differing views, and it is neither right nor wrong to be against G20 summits. It is perfectly natural that some people approve of it and some do not. And since when did this country disable people to speak freely of what they have in their minds? By adopting sound cannons, semi-weapons of mass destruction as some would call them, the government is drawing a clear and hostile line and treating citizens like potential terrorists or traitors. All the citizens want is to have their voices heard, and that is what the government should justly provide.

Adopting LRAD is not going to work well, but this does not mean that the police should do nothing ahead of the international summit. Instead, they should strive to develop more peaceful and democratic ways. Using sound cannons is no different from trying to exterminate any opposition by force. Shutting down the public's voice never brings about positive consequences. Before rushing for the means to silence the naysayers, the government should take some time to remind themselves that protesters are also their citizens, worthy of their protection.

Full of Passion
Korea University
Cheerleaders

The Korea University English Magazine

THE GRANITE TOWER(MARCH 2011)

By Park Shinji

Standing on the stage in front of 1200 students, their roar echoing in your ears, the game clock winding down, you shout out with what voice you have left, hoping it's enough to will the players on the field to victory. Following your lead, the students rise to their feet and begin chanting the "Boat Song" filling the stadium with Tiger spirit.

The Korea University(KU) Cheerleaders are in charge of cheering at KU. They represent KU and to present themselves in front of hundreds and thousands of students, they put in endless hours of practice.

The KU Cheerleaders are divided into three teams; the motion team, the music team, Elise, and the flag team, well known as the Young Tiger. The members of the motion team are the people we actually see on the stage in front of the stands. They lead the students in cheers and give encouragement to the teams and students. Elise, the band, plays music during school festivals and games. Last but not least, the flag team provides powerful performances with flags.

From freshman cheering orientation in March to the annual Ko-Yon games in September, KU Cheerleaders organize all the school festivals. Everything we see on stage is a result of their efforts off stage: choosing the time and place for the festivals, casting celebrities for Ipselenti "Jiya Hamsung" in May, and making new songs and routines for Ko-Yon games are their duties.

The spring semester is the busiest time for KU Cheerleaders. They have a lot to prepare: freshman membership training, KU cheerleading orientation, KU and Yonsei University(YU) joint cheerleading orientation, all in March, and the KU festival, Ipselenti, in May. They practice for hours to aim at perfection. The KU Cheerleaders meet from 9A.M. to 10P.M. every day during the vacation to practice and even during the semester they practice every morning and afternoon for 5 hours. These practice hours can be long and tiring but they are what bind the members as one. "We have a family-like atmosphere. And as we spend most of our time together, we actually feel like a family. We attend all the family occasions of our seniors as well." said KU Cheerleaders captain Lee Tae-Hoon('07, Philosophy).

When the bustling spring semester ends, it is yet another start of training for KU Cheerleaders, who now have the annual Ko-Yon games before them. One of their missions is to make a new cheer song with matching routine and present it at the annual Ko-Yon games. Last year, the new song was "GoGo Godae", which earned an explosive response for its cute motions. "When making a new song, to provide various satisfactions for KU students, we attempt to cover different music genres and try out new ideas," said the captain. "As for the motions, we first consider how students will accept the motions and then develop them. The different thing between KU cheering motions and that of other schools is that we focus more on motions that unite the students rather than motions that put emphasis on splendid performances."

The songs and motions are usually born only after thorough contemplations, but not always. Sometimes, fortuitous(adj. happening by chance, especially a lucky chance that brings a good result) opportunities lead to fresh and new discoveries. That is how the first hip-hop cheer "Onghaeya" was created. A cheerleading team member was supposed to bring the folk song version of "Onghaeya" but accidentally downloaded the hip-hop version. Yet, when they turned on the hip-hop version, it sounded novel and different. They gave the new version a try and it was a major success, earning great responses from students. Likewise, the idea for one of the cheering motions was created while members were just having fun. Mostly, the feelings of KU's cheer songs are majestic whereas the cheer songs of our rival, YU, are less powerful and cute. However, the trend seems to be slightly changing. "1 think that is because as both schools are trying to make something new, we are crossing over into each other's trends."

Many people believe that handling school work and cheerleading at the same time is not possible. Rumor has it that once you become a cheerleader, your grades go down. However, KU cheerleader members have proved the rumor wrong. "There are members who receive high grades that go above 4.0 GPA. It is not true that it is totally impossible to manage your grades as well as be a cheerleader. Mostly, it is up to you. Many members are living life to the full by doing well in school and practicing hard as a KU cheerleader," said Lee.

Despite many difficulties they may face as a cheerleader, they say the best part is meeting great people on the team. Going through everything together, the members become life-long friends. As a cheerleader, the best moments are when they see for themselves what they have worked for and feel fulfilled. "When the events go well and we see that we have made the students unite under the name of KU, we feel proud," said Lee. The sense of fulfillment also comes when the students really like the new song and all the efforts they have put into making it pay off. Not to be overlooked is the moment when the sports team turns the game around while leading the students' passionate cheers. Personally, the captain says he feels proud when he sees his juniors wearing the cheering uniform and proudly performing in front of the students.

For the upcoming 2011 semesters, KU cheerleaders are now preparing to soar again. Their key goal for 2011 is communication with the students. This year they hope to get closer to the students by keeping in step with them. Many things are in the process to do so. First, KU Cheerleaders just joined Twitter for better communication. Moreover, they are doing their best to make an application for the smartphones. Their homepage is being reorganized. The cheerleaders hope that their efforts will help resolve any misunderstandings or stereotypes about KU Cheerleaders.

Their wish this year is the active participation of all KU students. "It is sad to see the number of students participating in school festivals decrease. However, cheering for your school and feeling that sensation can be an once-in-a-lifetime experience. So I hope many students participate in the school festivals and feel the spirit of being a KU student."

Recruitment for freshmen KU Cheerleaders begins in March. The good news is that this semester, KU Cheerleaders are preparing a Recruiting Orientation on March 3 in the 4.18 Memorial Hall for those who want to join KU Cheerleaders. The members of KU Cheerleaders are planning to explain everything you need to know about being a cheerleader.

"Being able to do the cheering motions is not the most important factor in being a KU Cheerleader," says the KU Cheerleaders captain. "More than that, to be a cheerleader, you need to have the passion. Passion for the team, passion for cheering, and passion for your school is necessary. Nonetheless, talent is also important." To be accepted as a member, you need to pass an interview that mostly assesses your personality and how much you are willing to sacrifice for the school.

Passion seems to be the key factor in being a cheerleader. To endure the harsh training and to stand in front of thousands of students would not be possible without passion, devotion and pride towards what you are doing. Passionate mindsets and the confidence they gain as a cheerleader continue to work positively throughout their life. As a matter of fact, the former KU Cheerleaders, most of whom devoted their four years of university life to the KU Cheerleaders, excel in their fields after they graduate.

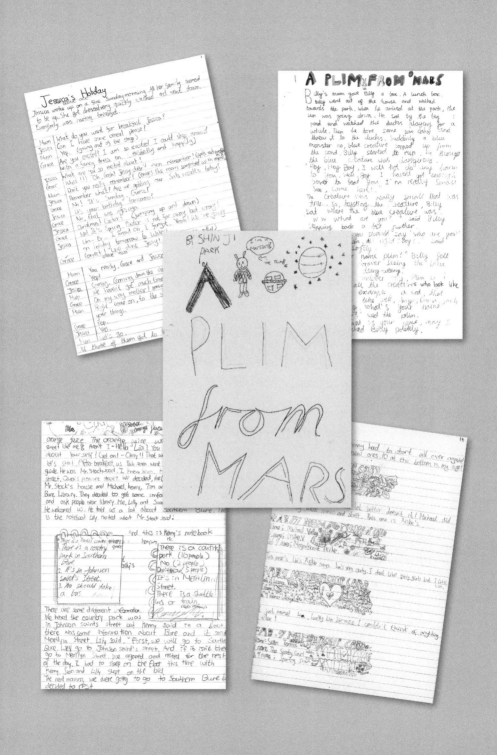

A PLIM from MARS

초판 1쇄 발행 2024년 12월 9일

지은이 ShinJi Park
펴낸이 강수걸
편집 이혜정 강나래 이선화 오해은 이소영 김효진 방혜빈
디자인 권문경 조은비
펴낸곳 산지니
등록 2005년 2월 7일 제333-3370000251002005000001호
주소 부산시 해운대구 수영강변대로 140 BCC 626호
전화 051-504-7070 | 팩스 051-507-7543
홈페이지 www.sanzinibook.com
전자우편 sanzini@sanzinibook.com
블로그 http://sanzinibook.tistory.com

ISBN 979-11-6861-395-9 03810